# REVELATION

IT WAS BEAUTIFUL. IT LOOKED LIKE ... IT LOOKED like ... Like ...

"There's nothing there," said Ethan Ring. The thing slipped from his field of vision like a glass eel. "I don't see anything."

"It's there all right," said Marcus Cranitch. Qwerty icons were summoned. "If I enlarge the image by a factor of ten ..."

The visual nothingness opened like a lotus blooming and engulfed them.

It was awe and it was wonder. It was beauty and it was terror. It was purity and it was judgment. It was everything and nothing, void and light, annihilation and creation. Alpha and Omega. The Primal *Fiat*. The Great I Am. It was love and truth and justice and holiness and might, everything every book, every verse, every mantra, every sutra said it was. It was every spiritual experience, every dervish dance, every glimmer of nirvana, every shaman trance, every elevation into rapture. It was more. Vastly more.

It was the face of God.

Other Bantam Books by Ian McDonald

The Broken Land
Desolation Road
Empire Dreams
King of Morning, Queen of Day
Out on Blue Six
Speaking in Tongues

# Scissors Cut Paper Wrap Stone

## IAN McDONALD

**BANTAM BOOKS**
New York   Toronto   London   Sydney   Auckland

Scissors Cut Paper Wrap Stone
A Bantam Spectra Book / February 1994

ISBN 0-553-56116-2

*Published simultaneously in the United States and Canada*

*Bantam Books are published by Bantam Books, a division of Bantam
Doubleday Dell Publishing Group, Inc. Its trademark, consisting of the words
"Bantam Books" and the portrayal of a rooster, is Registered in U.S. Patent
and Trademark Office and in other countries. Marca Registrada. Bantam
Books, 1540 Broadway, New York, New York 10036.*

PRINTED IN THE UNITED STATES OF AMERICA
RAD 0 9 8 7 6 5 4 3 2 1

Scissors Cut
Paper Wrap
Stone

THE BERLITZ-KIKOYAN SKULL-TAP GIVES ME IDIOMatic Tokyo-Bay argot, but the pilgrim's prayer, as ancient as the pilgrimage is long, defies easy translation: "Homage to Kobo Daishi, source of spiritual yearning, guide and companion on our quest." So much more elegant and simple in Japanese: *Namu Daishi Henjo Kongo;* easy on my lips as I kneel before the image in the Daishi Hall for the short preparatory ceremony. The muttered chains of repetitions, mantralike, slip between self and spirit, ease the excruciating self-consciousness of an over-tall, over-here Euro. With red hair. At an alien altar.

The first thing prayer changes is the pray-er, Masahiko—companion, guide, fellow pilgrim on this thousand-mile journey—tells me. And the last thing also. I hope so. I pray so.

There is no longer an incumbent at Temple One; a big Neo-Shinto shrine has wedged itself into the compound of the old Buddhist temple like a cuckoo chick into a sparrow's nest; its priest maintains grounds and buildings out of a sense of architectural and historical respect, but wary of offending the spirits, he does not assume any religious responsibilities. Our albums—the pilgrim's passport, to be stamped in vermillion with the official seal of each of the eighty-eight sacred sites—are marked by a coin-in-the-slot robot much in need of a new coat of paint. A sluglike feral zoomorph—brilliant yellow, with long trailing blue tendrils—feeds parasitically on the muscle-unit, tracking spirals of silver slime. The bright red stamp on the pure white paper is reassuringly exact, definite, bold, a statement of resolution. No going back now. We are committed. All the world knows the proverb that a journey of a thousand miles starts with a single step. What is not so widely known is that here, at Temple One, one takes that single first. Here also at Temple One is the last step, a thousand miles and eighty-eight temples later. Like the quest for enlightenment, the Shikoku pilgrimage is a circle, never beginning, never ending. Destinations are false goals; it is the Way Gone that matters.

We pause before the temple gate where we have left the bicycles to pay our respects at the Shinto shrine. The shrine is busy. Prayers for this, supplications for that, requests for healings, petitions for aid, for small, cybernetic miracles, for offenses to be pardoned and misfortunes lifted. It does not do to affront the simulacra of the ancestors. Linked through the Life Assurance Company AI matrix into the international datawebs, they can shovel a truly cosmic amount of shit your way. Religions, like pilgrimages, go in circles. As the Shingon Buddhism of Kobo Daishi—the saint in whose literal footsteps we follow—overwhelmed and absorbed primitive ninth-century Shinto, so twelve centuries later a renascent techno-Shinto of persona-simulation and soul-taps has pushed Buddhism into a seemingly terminal decline. What say the attenuated joys of nirvana against the recording and storing of memory, experience, and emotion with the hope of someday breaking through into true personality reconstruction?

Worshipers stare as we approach the massed banks of miniature television screens, each bearing the simula of some dear departed summoned back from informational limbo. Photographs, mementos, memorabilia, the toys, tricks, and trivia of living are epoxied to the television shells. The accepting, enfolding spirit of the Daishi Hall is shattered; my fears of being an alien in an alien place return redoubled. Masahiko reassures me. It is our white robes and sedge hats—the mark of a pilgrim, a *henro*—that are attracting attention. They are a rarity these days. Once thousands made pilgrimage each year; now if there are fifty geriatrics in a chartered coach it is a sign of mass spiritual revival. Once the ashes of the dead were taken to Mount Koya, across the Inland Sea in Wakayama Prefecture, Shingon's most holy place, to ensure rebirth in Amida's Pure Land in the West. Now on the local shrine anniversary, those insured with the big corporations come to have a year of recorded memory, emotion, experience downloaded from their soul-taps into the biocores.

I clap my gloved hands three times and run my yencard through one of the readers suspended on webbing straps from the lower branches of the cedars. At the beginning when everything can seem like an omen, you need all the good karma you can get. I wonder: Mas says that Japan's population has been falling steadily since the advent of soul-tap technology; have the life assurance companies accidentally created a dearth of spirits to be reincarnated?

As we leave the shrine an old woman comes pushing through the crowd in the gateway to press some small coins into our hands. She insists we accept. I am reluctant, Masahiko advises I take them. They are *settai*, pilgrim offerings; a tradition as old as the pilgrimage itself of bestowing small gifts upon henro: a few coins, like these, some summer fruit, a bowl of rice, a meal, a back massage. To refuse is pride. Humility of spirit is the Way of the pilgrim. Many of the ancient—and not so ancient—henro begged their way around the whole thousand miles. As etiquette demands, we give the old woman printed name slips. Mas's excites great interest, being a slip of ten-second smartplastic depicting Danjuro 19: *Kabukiman!*—his creation and Japan's number one *anime* superhero—transforming into one of his Classical Theater alter egos to battle evil. My humbler contribution is received no less thankfully: the old woman tells us the ceiling of her master bedroom is papered with henro name strips collected over several decades. Her continued physical vigor she attributes totally to their spiritual efficacy.

Outside the temple gate, we unlock the bikes. I check the bags—Mas's assurance that no one would dare steal under the gaze of the guardian deities who flank the gate, sifting souls, does not convince me. The demon box is where I left it, untampered with, untouched. Safe. Of course. But why does the best man at a wedding check his pocket for the ring every twenty seconds?

Ryōzen-ji's attendant town is busy; narrow streets overhung with neons and tattered plastic banners advertising European consumer electronics are crowded with trucks and pickups both hydrocarbon and muscle-powered. Smart market stalls and street vendors' booths hung with long, lovely vegetables—fed on nightsoil and artificial light until unbelievably huge and ripe—remind us that, despite the close-packed midrise emergency housing thrown up to accommodate refugees from the decaying offshore corporate arcologies, this is at heart farming country. We weave an uncertain course between darting biopower mopeds, their riders' eyes grim beneath helmets and smog masks. Massive, slow-moving tractor-trailer combines intimidate the roadside stalls and lean-to shelters of streetdwellers. Even in such company, we turn heads in our fluorescent MTB gear, white hip-length henro robes and inverted bowl-shaped henro hats clipped over safety helmets. The sedge hats are inscribed in quarters with the words of a very ancient, very Buddhist poem. As the urban drawl in my tap is not up to the highly Sinicized language of classical Japanese literary style, Masahiko translates:

> For the benighted: this world's illusions.
> For the enlightened, knowledge: all is vanity
> In the beginning was no east, no west,
> Where then, north and south?

Draw your own conclusions, pilgrim.

The henro's staff, bell, and stole that identifies him as a layman engaged on religious works we have had to forgo. Instead we have twenty-four-gear Day-Glo Dirt-Wolf freestyle MTBs hand-calligraphied by Masahiko with prayers and proverbs for the protection of travelers. Hard physical exertion and closeness to nature is an essential part of the pilgrimage: the God head in all things is the spirit of the Daishi's mountain Buddhism. That is why the most perfect way around the eighty-eight Sacred Sites has always been on foot. But in the post-industrial Japan of the second decade of the third millennium, Buddhism is in decline, the old path is impassable in many places, and the threat from bandits and power-armored *akira* gone AWOL from local security companies increases every year. We must cover long stretches of national highway, and inns and temple lodging houses are no longer numerous. On the terrain bikes we can honor the principle of achieving enlightenment by our own sweat and, where the path remains, follow the steps of the Daishi.

The steps of the Daishi. *Dogyo Ninin*: another pilgrimage proverb, painted by Mas on the front and rear shocks. We Two, Pilgrims Together. The belief has always been that Kobo Daishi walks at the side of each pilgrim, at times unseen, at others appearing in different forms and guises, occasionally manifesting himself in the full glory of his enlightenment. *Dogyo Ninin*. In honesty, the ideograms on our forks should read We *Three*, Pilgrims Together. Another shares the Daishi's place as invisible companion. Not by virtue of grace or enlightenment or any especially spiritual quality, but because of who she is, what she is.

I last saw her—unseen guest—in Capetown.

"Can't keep away from each other, can we, Eth?" After the Marrakech Room, her agency-ware had a decade's worth of industrials with tax-bucks to dump and commissions to offer stacked up. Maslow-Huitsdorp had outbid the competition (but then the Suid-Afrikan bioindustries could outbid almost anything except the European multinationals) and were weaning her off jet lag in the shadow of Table Mountain before taking her up to Bloemfontein to survey a site. As ever, I was a skulker in the shadows of the European Embassy, this party in the Kursaal where we met an attempt to woo the emergent black entrepreneurial caste away from Pan-Islam to Dame Europa's fiscal tit.

"Karmic cycles, Eth. It is predestined that our life paths cross and recross. Round we go, and round. In a previous existence we were probably Tom and Jerry." Her face had always held too much personality to be merely beautiful. Features wide, flat, scribbled by a child's crayon, ugly-beautiful, and that soft cockatoo crest of black hair that was always always always falling into her eyes. "Oh God, get me out of here. Everyone's so pretty and witty and gay. I need your uncompromising yeoman stodginess."

We walked on the beach, away from the stifling heat of the Kursaal. She slipped off her shoes and fastened them to her belt, let warm sand caress bare soles. The ocean fell and ran, fell and ran on the long beach.

"Atlantic or Indian, Eth? Where exactly does Atlantic end and Indian begin? If you're in a boat and cross the line, can you tell?"

Her entire life, it seemed then, had been made out of questions and considerations like those, of the peripheries of things.

"Heard from Mas?" she asked.

I told her that Danjuro 19: *Kabukiman!*, slayer of *ronin*, akiras, renegade robots, and Yakuza, Sword of Righteous Justice, et cetera, was now syndicated to fifteen Pacific Rim cable channels.

"Come a long way from a man, an *anime* deck, and a secret nocturnal vice," she said.

"He wants me to go on some crazy thousand-mile Buddhist pilgrimage with him," I said. "Says it would be good for my soul."

"He's probably right."

"He probably is." Even before Capetown, even before her, I had decided I would go. For my soul.

She took my hands in hers, studied them minutely. "No more kid-glove treatment, Eth?"

"Synthetic skin. Looks better. It comes off as easily as the gloves."

"That's what frightens me, Eth."

She let go of my hands, took my face between the palms of her hands, looked into my eyes. Gently but firmly she slapped me across the left cheek. Again and again and again, fitting her words to the tempo.

"Stupid stupid stupid boy. Always heroes and angels, isn't it, Eth?"

She stalked away toward the lights of the Kursaal. An International Fireworks Convention in town the same time as Europa's Three-Ring Diplomatic Circus was coming to a climax in the sky beneath Table Mountain.

"You're not fucking worth it, Ethan Ring. There only ever was you; is that not enough?"

In the morning the assignment was waiting for me on the room fax. I called at the desk to leave a goodbye, and an apology for her. The lobby was full of hung-over black businessmen hunting down breakfast. The white receptionist said she had left before dawn.


This first day of the pilgrimage we move up the Yoshino Valley, visiting each of the temples there and staying over at Temple Ten where the priest is a relation of a relation of a friend of Mas's. This is good farming land, a many-colored land: neat fields of yellow rape, purple clover, the sheer startling viridian of rice shoots, but mostly we make our way down footpaths and tractor tracks between tall, whispery groves of sugarcane. Near Temple Three we passed a big syrup factory; rural Japan seems to have adopted the biomechanical revolution more quickly and completely than the monstrous, decaying urban sprawls. The houses that we pass, the neat hamlets, the new villages, are all green-roofed, the engineered grass has the warmth and rusticity of the old rice thatch but never needs replacing. The few remaining sheet-metal roofs are garish and sharp-edged in comparison.

I do place and people a disservice to paint them as rustic characters. These quaint hamlets and villages are the heartland of the post-industrial revolution; each green roof sports a satellite dish to keep Juniors One Two Three in touch with the orbital EmTeeVee and sports channels, all along the valley construction teams from the big telecom companies are laying new fiber-optic cables. This is telecommuter land. Those casually dressed farmers who wave to us as we wheel past are the new caste of lawyers, doctors, accountants, designers, engineers, management consultants, near-space laborers, deep-sea miners. When Mas had a sebaceous cyst removed from his back, the only human he saw during the operation was the receptionist. The cyst had been excised by a teleoperator robot controlled by a surgeon three hundred kilometers away in a country manor among the green and pleasant golf courses of Shizuoka Prefecture. "Faith healing for agnostics," Mas calls it. When he called for his checkup, even the receptionist had been replaced by a suite of interactive software. "When it descends to sticking needles into holographic simulations of the patients to make them better, it'll really be cybernetic *macumba*."

Every Eden has its serpent. Among wage-earning

professional A-type males age thirty-five to fifty the most frequent cause of death is suicide, the second, exercise-induced coronaries. Death by volleyball. I suppose if I were Adam in a beautiful, perfect paradise where every need, every whim, was catered for, without change, without challenge, I might develop a taste for apple.

Wrong god. In Buddhism, what shit you get is of your own making. You don't inherit someone else's racial midden. The doctrine of Kobo Daishi's Shingon school is that any man may achieve enlightenment in this present life, not solely after struggling through countless thousands of painful incarnations. The Japanese have always been an optimistic people. You make your own karma.

The climb out of the valley to Temple Ten is steep. Thigh muscles throb and ache. After a long day in the saddle, we do not need this. It is as if the pilgrimage is testing our constitution and resolve: the way will only get harder; are you up to it, pilgrim?

Pilgrim drops down into low gear, grabs thrustbars, leans into pedals. I think I can I think I can I think I can . . .

I know I can.

The altar in the Daishi Hall of Temple Ten enshrines two images, both statues of Kannon, Boddhisattva of Mercy. According to temple legend, the first was carved by the Daishi from a living tree; the saint bowed three times before each stroke of the adze. The second is a woman weaver, a refugee from some Kyoto palace intrigue, who offered the saint a cut of her cloth—hence the name Kirihata-ji, Cut-Cloth Temple—to replace his ragged clothes. In reward for her piety a purple haze descended, and she was enlightened and transformed into a statue. After our devotions, Priest Mizuno shows us both images. I murmur with properly respectful awe, though both are crude, a few rough slashes in a wooden log. I suppose one must see with the eye of faith. The point, the priest tells us, is that anyone, including women—at the time an heretical notion, dogs had a better chance of gaining nirvana— may aspire to enlightenment.

After showering and freshening up, we dine with the priest's young family. His two sons, ten and twelve, are politely gobsmacked to be in the presence of the creator of *Danjuro 19: Kabukiman!* I am certain that the smartplastic *anime* slips Mas presents to them will be as enshrined and treasured as the Daishi's images of Kannon. After tea, Mrs. Mizuno announces that our baths are ready. As I have been expecting. As I have been dreading. On the pretext of blisters I return to our room and hunt for the synthflesh. For one heart-stopping moment I cannot find it among socks underwear shorts teeshirts weather-proofs, then my fingers close around its stubby, comforting cylinder. *This product dries to a flexible, porous, smooth finish in fifteen seconds,* say Hoffmann Helvetica Chemie Ag. Eyes firmly shut, I slip off my left glove, feel cool spray in the palm of my hand. I give it a double dose, just to be sure. Thirteen hippopotamus fourteen hippopotamus fifteen hippopotamus. Quick glance to make sure I am alone, then I close my eyes again, repeat the procedure for the right hand and go to join Mas and Mizuno, who, it transpires, is an old Soul fan. Up to our chests in hot, tangerine-scented water, we holler out Motown, Atlantic, and Stax classics in creaky three-part harmony. Mrs. Mizuno says it is the funniest thing she has heard in weeks.

The henro lodge is cool and airy, filled with the

sounds and scents of late spring in the Yoshino Valley. Sleep is easily found in such a room: within seconds I have tumbled into the slumber of the righteous.

When the cry wakes me I cannot think where I am for one hideous instant. I find my fingers tearing at the scab of artificial flesh in the palm of my right hand. No. No. *Namu Daishi Henjo*; I fight the demons with the weapons of a good pilgrim. And it passes.

Masahiko is bolt upright in his bed, eyes wide, body rigid, trembling. I can see that he is deep, far below the surface of his subconscious.

"Mas ..." Kneeling before him, I touch his shoulder, gently.

"No! No!" he shouts. "Leave her alone!"

"Mas?"

No answer.

"Mas ..."

No answer. I sit with him until whatever storm has troubled him has passed and he has settled back into sleep. I join him, we two, pilgrims together, and sleep without any further dreams until dawn.


The day is warm and bright as we splash across the gravel bed of the Yoshino River and follow the old henro path into the hill country. At Temple Ten valley Buddhism ends, mountain Buddhism begins. Zen is the spirit of the valleys, Shingon the spirit of the mountaintop. And as the spirit of Zen is different from the spirit of Shingon, so the sunlight and warmth of the valley give way to the more testing weather of the mountains. Gray wads of cloud move in from the west; within an hour it is raining steadily. Rain and mud, the henro's twin curses. Our legs are spattered with it, the bikes are caked with it, and our hands and faces are numb from cold rain. Rain sheets from our plastic capes and pilgrim hats. The way is steep and treacherous—bottom gear for an hour, with many portages. All head-on into wind and driving rain. Concentration is total. Misery absolute. Temple Eleven is deserted, derelict, decaying, vandalized by akiras. Among their graffiti, their beer cans, we find the remains of cooking fires, silver foil sachets of camping ready meals, condoms, needles, rotting biomotors and batteries, empty cartridges.

"I don't like this," says Mas, clearly spooked. Pigeons explode from beneath the eaves of the ruined Daishi Hall. Some, I notice, have parasitical zoomorphs clinging to their bodies. Reading it for an ill omen, we press on.

From Eleven to Twelve is half a day's ride past two *bangai*—unnumbered temples on the pilgrimage route that are not Sacred Sites. Both, like Eleven, are deserted and desecrated. On. Uphill all the way. I find my mind withdrawing, shutting out the sensual world and its insistencies, drawing veils of memory. I am no longer conscious of the cold and rain, the ache in my thighs. I remember.

I remember his life.

I call him "he" because, though he shared the same face, the same name, the same body and mind as I, he is dead. Unarguably. Indisputably. Dead. He was killed. Not with bullets or knives or monomolecular wire in an alley in some anonymous central European city, not with drugs or poisons. He was killed with guilt. What survived him, this thing pushing its gaudily colored MTB up the side of a Japanese mountain, is only the slag. Only the ashes.

I remember . . .

·　　　·　　　·

On the day that Ethan Ring was conceived, West Germany won the World Cup to the refrain of Luciano Pavarotti singing *Nessun Dormas* as Nikki Ring, twenty-something, unemployed, unemployable, engaged in five minutes of intense coitus in South Mimms Services car park off the M25 with a Dutch truck driver hauling a consignment of salad vegetables.

On the day that Ethan Ring was born an armor-piercing smartbomb hit an underground shelter in Baghdad and incinerated five hundred men, women, and children while Bette Midler sang about God watching us from a distance.

On the day that Ethan Ring kissed his first girl— Roberta Cunningham at the back of Miss MacConkey's P2 class—Europe very quietly, very unremarkably, without any embarrassing mess or fuss or anyone noticing, *united*.

On the day that Ethan Ring took his first date, Ange Elliot, age thirteen, to the local Pizza Hut for a double-cheese, diet Coke, and under-the-table footsie, Doctors ten Boom and Huitsdorp of the new, respectable, fully integrated, and racially harmonious South Africa won the Nobel prize for biology in recognition of their work on designing an artificial organism that converted sugars into useful electricity—to layman Ethan and his contemporaries, a living battery.

Too tall too early, red hair—too much of it— socially crippled by acne and self-consciousness, Ethan Ring would almost certainly have grown into neurotic teenhood but for the shelter, succor, and support of the Nineteenth House kinship. From the moral ruins of the HIV-haunted nineties, strewn with the desiccated bones of broken relationships, a new sociological order had emerged of clusters of single women—separated, widowed, divorced, never partnered—joined together under a common roof against a sea of free-floating males. The kinship: average size five point three: three point two generating the income to support themselves and the average two point one career mothers who parented the children. Men come, men go at the individual partners' discretions, but are never considered part of the family unit. 2003: the kinship achieves legal recognition in the European courts. 2012: one third of all permanent relationships are kinships. 2013, early May: Nikki Ring joins the Nineteenth House gaining a telecommuting designer of European farming magazines, a home-delivery sandwich Empress, a jewelry maker, a co-mother who has retired thankfully into parenthood out of Futures, two new daughters, one new son, a condominium on the South Coast (the eponymous Nineteenth House) with sun terrace and shared swimming pool, peace, stability, love, security; contributing: Ethan Ring. Ethan Ring gained roots; he whose prior experience of the New Europe had been Doppler blur of taillights punctuated by ten thousand radio jingles and the smell of scorched sunflower oil in a nation of bed'n'breakfast rooms. The fertile ground of the kinship germinated a long-dormant talent for *visualization*, for seeing ideas projected on the backs of his eyeballs and making them seeable to other others. Nurtured by his ex-Futures co-mother, his talent took him through and out of Michael Heseltine Comprehensive to art college in some rainy day city in the north to study Graphic Communications. He suffered agonies of acclimatization and socialization. He contemplated leaving. He contemplated a bottle and a half of paracetamol. He found friends in time: a Japanese exchange student with a dark and secret passion for comic-book animation; a dark-haired computer junkie from the North Country who taught Ethan the necessary skills of drinking rolling joints pulling girls; his girlfriend, a fellow Graphic Communications student who looked as if her name should end with a "y" but in fact didn't.

On the day that Ethan Ring met Luka Casipriadin, Leconte Bio in Lyons discovered a technique for loading human memories, emotions, and experiences from an implanted bioprocessor onto a mainframe AI template to create an interactive simulacrum of the dead. The first immortal since ancient Greece came from Santa Rose, CA, had Made It in sugar beet, but couldn't beat the carcinoma. Her persona was alone three years in cybernetic heaven before anyone could afford to join her.

Somebody had stolen Ethan Ring's shopping. He had gone back to lock up his rustbucket of a Ford and the bags were gone from outside his first-floor flat. Life in the rainy-day city had made him stoical: microwave TVchow-4-1s made him fat and gave him wind anyway. The next day there was a knock at his door. On the landing was the girl from first-year Fine Arts you could not help noticing because she had shaved her head except for a crest of black hair that flopped into her eyes all the time.

"You could at least have made some effort."

"Pardon?"

"Knocked a few doors. Made a few routine inquiries. You could have tried a little."

"I'm sorry. Are you sure you've got the right flat?"

"Okay okay, I admit it. I took your food. Me. Luka Casipriadin. I live upstairs from you. You didn't know.

Ah. It's Georgian, originally. Casipriadin. So my father says. Can I come in?"

"You took my food? Why did you take my food?"

But she was already sitting on his curry-and-beer-stained sofa scrutinizing with the eye of first-year Fine Arts his soft-porn posters of airbrushed cyber-girls with chromium breasts. Shit shit shit piles of dirty underwear Chinese food cartons beer cans.

"One life furnished in early squalor. You know you are what you eat?"

"Unh?"

"I'm beginning to think maybe I made a mistake with you. Syllogismic logic: if I am what I eat, and you are what you eat, then if I eat what you eat, therefore I should become you."

"So you ate my food."

"And got fat and farted a lot."

"Why ..."

"Because you have fabulous hair I would kill for. Because you were never going to talk to me, so I had to get to talk to you. You hungry? Of course you are. I ate all your food. Come up to my place. I've got stuff on."

"My stuff?"

"My stuff. Eat my food, be me. You have a name?"

"Ethan Ring."

"Oh, classic name. I knew I hadn't made a mistake with you."


From the perspective of a fluorescent speck clinging to a mountainside in Shikoku, I am able to tell her that she had, she did, a small mistake, a misjudgment of character, that would slowly, gradually, destroy entire lives. Sensitive dependence on initial conditions; one word, one act, can change the world. Well they named it *chaos theory*.

From the perspective of the pilgrim, this mountain land is exhilarating; the swoop from the mountaintop temples down the sheer henro path is thrilling, madly reckless. There is a great spirit in high country. Shinto peopled the peaks with ancestors and kami but clung to the valleys; Buddhism took its temples to the very mountaintops and opened the numinous to the people of the valleys. The legends attached to Shikoku's high places gives an indication of the power of the spirit of the mountains in the Japanese psyche.

A hundred years before Kobo Daishi, En the Ascetic, an early Buddhist missionary, bound a fire-breathing dragon that had been ravaging the farms and livelihoods of the people below beneath a stone on the hilltop where Temple Twelve now stands—the temple to which we are traveling along forest trails and fire-breaks. Inspired by the Buddha, the boy Daishi went up to the mountain peaks above the valley of his birth—a subtemple of Temple Seventy-five commemorates the spot—and leapt from the summit, crying out, "If I am to be the people's savior, then save me, O Buddha! If not, then let me perish!" Naturally, Buddha erred on the side of mercy. To me the most meaningful legend of mountain Buddhism is that of Emon Saburo; a rich and oppressive landlord from Ehime Prefecture (a valley man, short in spirit) who shat in the begging bowl of a wandering priest—the Daishi in disguise—and thus earned the Job-like curse of losing family, friends, and fortune in a single night. Smitten by conscience, he gave all his lands to his tenants and set off in pursuit of the Daishi to beg forgiveness. But however strenuously he pursued the saint, he was never able to catch up with him. After four years and twenty circuits, he was struck by the idea that he would stand a better chance of meeting the Daishi if he reversed the direction of his pilgrimage and so met him coming. On his twenty-first circuit of Shikoku he came, near to death with cold and exhaustion, to a mountaintop. The Daishi appeared to him and absolved him of his sins. Before dying, Emon Saburo requested that he might be reborn as the lord of his home province—then Iyo, now known as Ehime—so that he might do mighty works of good to atone for his evil deeds in this life. The Daishi picked up a small stone, wrote Saburo's name on it, and pressed it into his hand. Then Emon Saburo died and the Daishi buried him and changed his pilgrim staff into a cedar.

Like all good stories, there is a twist in the tale. Late the next summer, the wife of the Lord of Iyo gave birth to a son; fine, healthy, beautiful, except that his left hand was clenched shut and could not be opened. A Shingon priest was summoned, who prayed and invoked the name of the Daishi over the boy. Slowly, his fist relaxed, and opened. Inside was a small stone. On the stone were written the words "Emon Saburo Reborn."

*Namu Daishi Henjo Kongo!*

We ride up the long, shallow steps to Temple Twelve. No priest here, nor any pilgrims; we share the mountainside forest clearing with a handful of industrial robots marked with the ciphers and seals of Tokushima Prefecture Bureau of Antiquities. Beyond Twelve the gray weather breaks. Unfaltering sunshine lights our way and we go ridgerunning across the tops of the valleys and down the mountain paths. Light has always made me feel reborn. I want to do this forever.

Temple Thirteen—Dainichi-ji—is sited on a coll at the head of a valley of big, prosperous farmhouses set like scattered islands in a sea of gently undulating sugarcane and bamboo. Like Twelve, it has fallen from grace, staffed also with stolid robots in the employ of the Bureau of Antiquities. Prayers in an empty hall; a computer stamps our albums. As we click into our toe clips, lean into handlebars, a Nissan biopower pickup pulls up outside the gate in a crunch of damp gravel. A middle-aged woman with startling fluorescent green rubber boots leaps out and greets us warmly. Her name is Mrs. Morikawa. She owns a farm ten kays down the valley, but is also the official curator (part-time) of Buddhist Cultural Heritage Sites Twelve–Fifteen. Her monitors flagged her that there were henro working their way along the old pilgrim path: we are the first in three years to have followed the Daishi's Way, would we do her the honor of staying the night as guests in her farmhouse?

We consider her offer of settai. The afternoon is almost gone. Temples Fourteen and Fifteen are eight kays distant over heavy terrain. Mas has booked us into a drab tourist motel just outside Tokushima on the main interprovincial highway. Waiting is a warm farmhouse, country food, clean beds, hot water.

The bikes go in the back, we squeeze into the front beside Mrs. Morikawa. Gunge-tacked to the dash is a mass-produced plastic statue of the Daishi in henro robes. *Dogyo Ninin.*

As we drive through the cane plantations and bamboo, Mrs. Morikawa confesses an ulterior motive behind her gift of hospitality. Her eldest daughter is sick with an unnamed wasting disease. The doctors and their robots have offered the most advanced medical science but they admit that sicknesses such as these are as much of the spirit as of the body. She wonders: could we, would we, see her daughter? Ancient belief credits great power to the temple seals inscribed in henro albums; Mrs. Morikawa and her mother before her saw great acts of healing when pilgrims passed their albums over the bodies of the sick. Mas protests: we are not faith healers, miracle workers, shamen, *hijiri*—itinerant Buddhist holy men—we are spiritual seekers sinful as any men. We do not emulate the Daishi, merely follow his way. The woman pleads—it can do no harm. Indeed, it cannot, nor any good, if it is only a matter of calligraphy passed over a sick spirit. But I feel, I know, that it may be more. Must be more. Demons and Daishis are jealous masters where spirits are at stake. Wind stirs the tall bamboo and in the space of a few sentences the dirt road with its twists and turns has become the entrance to a moral trap so intricate, so labyrinthine, I am its captive before I am aware I have entered.

"We will do it," I say, cutting Mas's protests short. Mrs. Morikawa is overjoyed.

Grass roof sloping nearly to the ground, satellite dishes, comlinks, shit digesters, methane plants, syrup tanks, agricultural robots: a typical twenty-first-century Japanese country manor. A son leaves off easing the dead biomotor out of a roboplanter to store the bikes in the barn. Halfway to the house something hits me a huge, soft thump in the back. As I go sprawling on the concrete the woman picks up a black, flapping something, shouts at it, throws it away from her. With a scream of indignation, it scuttles into the barn.

A glider cat.

The woman apologizes. They recently bought a franchise. Now every time anyone calls at the house, they come swooping down from high vantages on the webs of furred skin between their fore and hind legs to investigate. As she opens the door, a black ball of fur crouched above the porch opens moon-yellow eyes and regards us balefully.

The smell of death in the sick girl's room is so strong as to be almost overpowering. It is not easily learned, but once you have the stink of it, it never quite leaves you. I cling to the door frame to steady myself.

"Won't eat, won't talk, won't let anyone help her, won't do anything but lie in her bed and swallow pills," says Mrs. Morikawa in the voice of a woman so accustomed to pain it has become an intimate friend.

The girl is fifteen, sixteen, the age it likes its victims best. Anorexia, bulimia, cognitive metabolic disorder; they have found new names and faces for it but at its heart its name has always been self-loathing, its face, self-destruction. The doctor who called it a disease of the spirit advised well. Mas swears quietly, reverently in English.

A television with a hand-sized Sony camcorder clipped to it stands on a corner shelf. Onscreen twenty-two men in shorts chase a black and white checkered ball about an astroturf field. In the bottom right corner, two faces, an old man and an old woman. The simulas of dead grandparents, keeping watch on their beloved granddaughter from Amida's Pure Land in the West through the little Sony camera. Seeing henro in their field of vision they smile and bow to us from beyond life.

If the girl notices us as we hold our albums over her and offer prayers she makes no response. Mrs. Morikawa seems satisfied and thanks us for our time and prayers. The Daishi will save her daughter. She has faith. A faithless *gaijin*, I feel guilty, fraudulent, an itinerant rainmaker, a wandering snake-oil seller.

Over pork chosenabe—we use an old Buddhist euphemism of calling wild boar "mountain whale" to subvert meatlessness—Mrs. Morikawa's three sons and younger daughter question us about the pilgrimage. If they recognize Mas they are too well brought up to pester him with Kabukiman questions. Cakes are served, and tea. The youngest boy fetches in a big pallet of beer cans. Considering himself excused from the injunction against alcohol because he has performed a virtuous deed, Masahiko drinks freely. The others join him only out of politeness. I decline. There is a pain in my stomach. It is not muscle cramp, it is not a foreign devil's misreaction to Mrs. Morikawa's pork chosenabe. It is the sharp-hooked horn of dilemma twisting in my guts. I can save myself and damn. I can damn myself and save.

"And Mr. Morikawa?" Mas asks, made overconfident by 8.5 percent proof.

"Dead these three years past," Mrs. Morikawa says. "He died up at Temple Eleven. Akiras had taken over the Temple; he could not stand the thought of them turning one of Shikoku's Sacred Sites into a latrine. He was a stupid man in many ways, but not so stupid as to go up against them alone. Then Tosa Securities bought out the policing contracts to the valley and as a gesture of goodwill mounted an offensive against bandits and petty warlords upcountry, including the akira chapter at Temple Eleven. It was terrible; we could hear the shooting all the way down in the valley. We could see the muzzle flashes the tracers. Eventually, my husband could not stand by and listen to them destroying his Temple anymore. He went up there to try and talk sense into them. A ToSec enforcer shot him by mistake for an akira, even though he had a white flag with him. It had only been two months since his last download; they took his tap across the Inland Sea to the Osaka Number Eleven simulator. He grew up near there. This year the premiums are up twenty percent and ToSec are sending their enforcers to every household to encourage prompt payment."

To follow as a pilgrim in a master's footsteps leaves you no choice over which way to go. You do as he would do, no matter the pain.

With apologies, I leave the somber little party for the barn. The lights come on automatically; curious kittens peep from the hayloft and come swooping down on their wings to alight on the floor beside me, rubbing and purring. It is exactly where I left it in the bottom of my left-hand bag. The organic batteries are still strong and there is a new cartridge of biodecay paper in the printer. Because any words of mine would only frighten and confuse, I say none and slip past the big farmhouse kitchen to the sick girl's room. No witnesses: I switch off television and 'corder, banish grandpa and grandma to cybernetic limbo. Moths dance on the window glass. By the light of the moon, I set up the demon box.

FRACTER GENERATION SYSTEM LEVEL THREE INTER-FACED, says the demon box.

My fingers hesitate for a moment over the Qwerty symbols on the flat black face of the box. Like that other box in the legend, once this is opened, what comes out cannot be put back again.

TIFERET, I type, one slow letter at a time.

COMMIT CODE?

WHAT I TELL YOU THREE TIMES IS TRUE.

The screen blanks. My mouth is dry.

PASSWORD VALIDATED. VISUAL DISPLAY OR HARDCOPY?

HARDCOPY.

The printer shrieks. I peel off the backing strip, stick the adhesive slip to the television screen, swivel an anglepoise to illuminate the thing printed on it, and go to the side of the bed.

"Come on, daughter," I say in English. "Time for thine eyes to see the glory of the coming of the Lord." With my back to the chaotic un-geometries of the fracter, I open her eyelids with my thumbs.

No audible response, no tactile change beneath my fingertips. But her pupils dilate. She sees. And being seen, the fracter slips past the defenses of her conscious-ness into the primal presentient core of neurochemical reaction.

Minutes pass, slow, stretched, time-dilated. Her eyes close, she slips back into sleep. I am no medico, but I know the difference between this and the shallow, rest-less drowse from which I woke her.

Voices in the landing. Mas, Mrs. Morikawa. The bedroom door opens, a crack, a line of yellow light. They cannot see what I am doing here. I slam the door, turn the deadlock.

"Ethan?"

"Leave me, Mas. I can help her, trust me."

"Mr. Ring?"

"It will be all right, Mrs. Morikawa. I will not harm her, I swear. Just give me this one night. Please."

This has always been the way with the fracters: evil sown with the good. With healing and wholeness, sus-picion and mistrust. What other choice did I have but to make them mistrust me? I find a chair out of the line of sight, to sit, to wait. Nightwatch. The clustered lights of the low-orbital manufactures arc slowly overhead and I remember the life of Ethan Ring.

All her major decisions, she said, were made by contrail-o-mancy. Jet trails. Inbounds, outbounds, conjunctions, and near-misses. Hexagrams of the heavens. "Make a lot more sense than leaves, cards, and bones. Divination should be a product of its time. It's only logical."

"What do you do on cloudy days?" he asked.

"Cloudy days I don't even get out of bed."

At which precise moment an outbound trans-polar suborbital made a perfect thirty-two-degree trine with an inbound shuttle from Frankfurt and he fell in love with her. Having never fallen in love before, it was a pleasure to discover that *falling* was the most precise description language could offer of the sudden, shocking emotional vertigo he felt. It terrified him. It thrilled him. It was like being handed the keys to the best ride in the fairground and told to play until dawn. Thoughts of her crept unasked into every stray moment, kept him warm and horny.

"So when are you going to do something about it?" asked Masahiko the *anime* hero and Marcus Cranitch the computer junkie and his girlfriend who looked as if her name should end in a "y" and was in fact called 'Becca and all the drinkers thinkers jokers poseurs bozos bimbos nymphos and boyos who comprised first-year B.A. Hons Graphic Communications, who had collectively and individually noticed that Luka Casipriadin was climbing the five flights of stairs between Fine Arts on one and Design on six at least four times a day.

"Do something?" said Ethan Ring, who had never

considered the possibility that so splendid a creature could reciprocally love him.

"Do something!" thundered Masahiko Marcus 'Becca-without-the-Y and the drinkers thinkers jokers poseurs bozos bimbos nymphos and boyos.

She came knocking on his apartment door one Tuesday winter evening, waltzed into his kitchenette space, and while washing down fistfuls of Rice Krispies with milk from the bottle ("They snapcracklepop on your tongue") said, "Got something to show you. Come on," and shoved him into a waiting taxi.

"Where?"

"Here."

She unloaded a computer from the front seat, paid the driver.

"But there's nothing here." His breath steamed in the damp November cold. Spirited out without even a grab for a jacket, he shivered and wrapped his long orang-utan arms around him for warmth.

"Yes there is. A building site is here. Not any building site, but the building site for the Wildwood Center, no less; the Numero Uno Leisure Shopping Development in the Industrial Northwest."

"A building site."

"Yeoman." She waved. In his glass security cabin bolted to the steel exoskeleton of Wildwood, the nightwatchman waved back. Razor-wire-topped metal gates slid open on creaking rollers.

"Shall we?" Bank by bank, section by section, yellow floodlamps kicked on, throwing planes and shafts of light and shadow across the rectilinear frame of girders and floors.

"Fucking hell," said Ethan Ring.

"It's not what you know, it's who you know." Luka

showed him into a service elevator. "But not in the biblical sense." Up: ten twenty thirty meters into the grid of light. "Fourth floor; ladies foundation garments, rubber hosiery, and exotic millinery." She ducked under the safety gate, pulled Ethan after her into an Escheresque dimension of concrete horizontals interrupted by support piers and prefabricated walls. In places floors and ceilings were incomplete; yawning voids opened and overlapped onto lower levels; above, the cold November sky, threatening rain. The unavoidable debris of Construction Man lay scattered about ("You should hear some of the propositions I've had"); his tools, his toys, his topless Page Three girls, his diet Coke cans.

Luka unhooked a wraparound VR audio-visualizer and paired datagloves from her belt and handed it to Ethan Ring.

"Watch and learn, lover."

The lift into altered perception was terrifying and thrilling.

Planes and shafts of stabbing color, curves, angles, all connected by rushing lines of force, of velocity. The sense of *speed* as he moved across the concrete floor sent him reeling. Air compressors, welding equipment, power tools, portable generators, became vibrant vortices of movement. He could *see* the energy they contained as a rush of images, time dependent action compressed into static timelessness. A discarded bottle opened up into spirals and planes of stored power; a crumpled newspaper became a whirling concatenation of information and vertigo.

"What is this?" he begged, seeking stability, seeking Luka, seeing a blur of kinesis.

"The Boccioni-verse." Her voice was a deep, sure root in the hurtling instability. "Umberto Boccioni;

doyenne of the Italian Futurist painters, 1882–1916; obsessed with industry, energy, velocity, and aggression. This place is perfect for him. 'The City Rises'! Can't you just smell the testosterone? Would have made a great fascist if he hadn't fallen on his head while out riding one morning in Verona and prematurely terminated himself."

The slightest movement of his head sent lines of colored energy rushing past him.

"How do you do this?"

"With computers. Isn't everything? I remixed an old video image-processing system using retailored commercial enzyme programs to hack it apart and reassemble it." Shedding planes of hand-shaped light, she picked up a fiber-optic cable, burning, writhing with visible information. "Head-mounted cameras pick up images, the mobile here processes them and feeds them back to the VRs. This one's visual-only mode. Later I may add extra dimensions. Next, I'm thinking, maybe a Cubistverse, or even Kandinsky. Miro, perhaps? You fancy me as a squiggly black thing with a little blobby head? Eventually, I want to create my own discrete, personal universes. Luka-verses like no one's ever seen before. Found sources. Junk aesthetics. Reality overdubs.

"They can't see it, Ethan. The others in my class. Because I want to use software remixing to mold reality/virtuality overlays, I'm a fascist. Mechanistic, soulless, irrelevant to the zeitgeist of twenty-first-century man trapped in a universe of quantum indeterminacy, they say. But at least I care. I love what I do, I love why I do it; I'm not tapping my forehead three times in the shit to Ideology-of-the-Month. They care about their P.C. credibility, or being talked about by the right set, or mentioned by the right tutors, or if they're tutors themselves, at the right parties, fuck integrity, fuck originality, fuck *art*. I care, Eth. I care like fuck, and I want someone to know it." Her voice, speaking from the heart of a whirlwind of cascading images, held a dark, tightly focused savagery Ethan Ring found disturbing and exciting for the same reasons.

Mechanistic soulless irrelevancies to the zeitgeist notwithstanding, she received a Distinction for the Boccioni-verse project and persuaded Ethan to throw a celebration party in his flat.

"What's wrong with yours?" he asked.

"Ah!" was her only answer.

Everyone from his and her classes who was not too small-spirited to accept turned up. They danced badly to far too loud music. They drank far too much. They smoked atrocious things and popped worse. They behaved abominably in public at antisocial hours, reeling up and down the street on each other's shoulders, falling on cars, denting bodywork, setting off a Stockhausen symphony of security alarms. All night he watched her moving around his flat talking, laughing, drinking, grinning, looking beautiful and brilliant in a head-turning rubber dress, surrounded by brilliant beautiful drinking laughing talking people as irresistibly drawn to her as he in a cordon he could not penetrate for one word, one laugh, one dance for himself. Returning from the bathroom—so full of dope smoke it disconnected its many visitors from reality as effectively as any of Luka's virtuality overdubs—he met her in her breathtaking rubber dress filling in clues on the World's Longest Crossword that ran all the way around his living/ sleeping room into the kitchenette space.

"Ethan." Her fingers on his arm were *urgent* in a way he had never felt before. "Come on." She pulled him away from the World's Longest Crossword, away from the party, up the stairs to her flat. "Come *on*." Into her bedroom. "Three parallel outbounds this evening. A crux, a crisis, a point of transition. This is the time." She pulled him to her. She smelled of whiskey, warm rubber, and wild wild things. "Why do you think I had the party down in your place?" She locked the door. "Welcome to the Luka-verse."

The voice wakes me. For the second it takes the tap to download I cannot understand; then glass pyramids of language crystallize in my mind.

"Please, I'm so hungry, can't I have something to eat?"

Dull gray light in the window; dawn light. She is so weak and frail she can hardly hold herself upright in the bed. The dull deathliness is gone from her eyes. There is a new light in her.

My ribs ache, the backs of my knees throb from having fallen asleep with my feet propped on the dressing table. Head like a loaf of stale bread, mouth like Satan's rectum. Before I destroy the evidence of my dark art, I permit myself one brief glance.

Tiferet: Angel of Healing and Wholeness.

*Well-being* cascades through my *chakra* centers from the top of my head to the soles of my feet. Muscular aches and nags are wiped away. I feel I can run a marathon, outspring a greyhound, leap tall buildings in a single bound. I feel Olympian. I feel immortal.

"Please, mister, something to eat?"

I go out into the hall and call for Mrs. Morikawa. The house is awake within seconds. I gain the impression that no one has been asleep. While Mrs. Morikawa and family run about filled with joy, preparing miso soup, sloppy rice, tea, I wake Mas.

"The girl?"

"She'll be all right now."

He is still drunk with sleep.

"What ... how?"

"Later. I promise." What have I forced myself into? What lies, what deceptions, what mistrusts and hurts? A spiritual searcher would pray Lord Daishi for grace to save him from the consequences of doing right, but I am only doubting, profane Ethan Ring. "We should get going if we want to be on the far side of Tokushima City by nightfall."

"It's twenty past five in the morning."

"I know."

I want to be on the henro path and over the next mountain before the Morikawas, after rejoicing, remember us, and want to thank us, praise us, give us things. Ask us questions. Bikes are ready, packs prepared in half an hour. With the light coming up all around us, pouring into the valley, flooding over us, we climb up through the bamboo and cane groves toward the henro way, me leading, Mas close up on my rear wheel.

From the high farming country we dip down again onto the densely populated coastal plains. Many temples here, much traffic inbound for Tokushima. No place for the uninterrupted cultivation of memory. The way demands total concentration. Tokushima City, the prefectural capital, is noisy, dirty, nasty; straining to the point of collapse under the weight of migrants from the failed offshore colonies and the social chaos of the Tokyo Bay conurbation. Tokushima is—always has been—a barrier gate city. In historical times, the borders between provinces were tightly policed, and barriers established to check on the authorization and travel permits of traders and visitors. Henro were barely tolerated, suspected of being spies, assassins, Imperial agents, or other undesirables. Alongside the political barriers existed a second kind of barrier gate: temple barriers, places of spiritual examination and testing, where the pilgrim who was able to worship freely and purely might continue, but if misfortune was encountered, or ill omen, he must return and begin his pilgrimage again.

The political barriers may have fallen, but the spiritual gates still stand. The henro path takes us away from Tokushima City's thronged main thoroughfares, through back streets and industrial districts where the now-permanent recession that has struck down Japan is everywhere visible, the closed-up shops, the shut-down small factories. Mass-produced accommodation pods stacked ten, twenty high pen us in, direct us into a labyrinth of lanes and alleys. Emergency housing; the estate of the new dispossessed. Mas is visibly uneasy; even I can sense the angry desperation, one freakish alien among two hundred million; more, I am of that people that challenged and defeated their empire and condemned them to the estate of refugees in their own country. Children in This Year's Model sportsgear watch with a disturbingly adult intensity from the scramble nets and bamboo ladders that access the higher levels; men squat at intersections around boomboxes, play handball against graffiti-stained walls, hang about, hang out, wait; women are the salarypersons here, casual part-time workers in labor-intensive service industries. Only the biopowered robots have jobs for life with the compassionate the caring the Company. Smells of shit, charcoal, street food, engine oil, hot dust, and the undefinably familiar sweet scent of home-brew E-Base.

Sounds of twenty satellite channels playing at once; in every stall, every bar, every shop, every home, robot-manufactured flatscreen Sonys play all day, play all night. Life during prime-time. Disemboweled vehicles. Shot-down streetlights. Abandoned shopping trolleys. Graffiti aspiring to be Art, and Noticed. Dogs—fighting dogs.

For some people it is the hairs on the back of the neck. For others, the pricking of the thumbs. For me, it has always been a tingle at the base of my spine; that unmistakable prescience of *trouble*. Eight of them, in light camouflage armor set to Chapter heraldics, enfolded by the elaborate streamlines of techno-gothic Yamahas. Akiras: middle-class kids seduced away from teleburbia's low-key pleasures by fifteen channels of samurai-*anime* cut with the Guitarz'n'Blood ethos of Trash Metal, fleeing from a mythologized Imperial past, questing for an unattainable future. The big Yams circle us; engines growl, gobbling hydrocarbons. On the pillion seats, girls with fluttering standards fixed to the backs of their jackets analyze us with scanshades, intimidate us with black lip gloss. A word from the leader—a fat, dangerous youth who has solved a terminal greasy hair problem by knotting it into a queue—and they hustle us into dark and stinking ratrun between overlapping levels of housing pods. His blackseat girl plays with my red hair, twines it around her black leather fingers, sucks it between her wet black lips. Mas, an uncharacteristic tone of panic creeping into his voice, bows constantly, spastically, repeating that we are only pilgrims following in the footsteps of the Daishi, two innocent pilgrims. Fat Boy would rather stare at the impudent red-haired *gaijin*. His hand strokes to my neck; I flinch away. A silent flash lights up the inside of my skull, a numb dumbness; my language tap has been ripped out of its socket. He tosses it end for end, catches it in his gloved hand. Mas's pleadings now verge on breaking down completely, and the words have been literally taken out of my mouth. Fat Boy is irritated. With people like these, irritated is dead. I have seen it, I know. And I know that I must act, though the henro in me screams at the thought of releasing the demons ... I shout to Mas in English: *Close your eyes. Now. Do as I say!* and reach to peel the glove off my right hand. A steel whisper: the girl whips a short *tachi* from a sheathe on her thigh, presses the tip to my Adam's apple. I raised my hands, gloved. Head cocked gaminely to one side, she is smiling. Fat Boy is smiling. His friends are smiling.

If irritated is dead, smiling is gutted. Smiling is head on a jacket-back pennant-stay. A shout. Fat Boy's deputy has found something in Mas's bags. The commander clicks his fingers *show me*. It is one of Masahiko's Danjuro 19: *Kabukiman!* henro slips! Fat Boy holds it up before Mas's face, raps questions. Even without my tap, their context is clear from Fat Boy's intonation and Mas's terrified, nodded answers. Then with the same terrifying speed with which it was drawn, the sword is resheathed. Fat Boy bows, returns me my tap, bows to Mas, and offers him the henro slip deferentially, with both hands.

"Kabukiman? You make Kabukiman?" He turns to his gang and shouts theatrically. "He! Invented! Danjuro 19!" His platoon murmur and bow, genuinely awed. "The Setting Sons Chapter owes you a big apology, both of you," says Fat Boy. The transformation is so swift and staggering I still cannot believe it. "We've treated men on spiritual business dishonorably. Tosa Securities is expanding into Tokushima Holdings territory;

they're trying to win policyholders over by looking strong against the brothers. Tokushima Holdings is fighting back and the street is in the middle. The Black Dragon Chapter was wiped out last month; you can't trust anyone anymore. They've got agents everywhere. Can you forgive us? At least let us escort you to the next temple; we'd be proud to do that for the creator of Kabukiman."

We can hardly refuse. Pennants fluttering and tugging, wing mirrors glinting, the akiras mount up and form vanguard and rearguard around us. The sound of the Yamahas reverberates from the housing stacks and the recession-struck, shuttered-up businesses. On the faces of the people that we pass I see who are the back-street heroes, the Young Soul Rebels, the Robin Hoods to the big Police Corporations' Sheriffs of Nottingham and Guy of Gisbornes. Fat Boy, riding close beside, tells me that, to them, Kabukiman is the spirit of true Japan, epitome of honor, justice, respect, individuality, faithfulness, action, experience, and violence; the measure of a real man. "He knows how to live," Fat Boy says. His girlfriend reaches out to touch my hair, run it over her black glossy fingers.

"Hey, mister with the fabulous hair, Danjuro 19 was always the friend of the true akiras," she says.

At Temple Eighteen we make our ablutions and devotions and have our albums inscribed while the akiras lounge about on their bikes outside the temple gate, smoking. The priest wants to call Tosa Securities, I dissuade him. Fat Boy accepts the Kabukiman henro slip with tears in his eyes and gives us each a pack of Black Cats as settai. Later, I say, when the pilgrimage is over and we can enjoy such things, we will smoke them and think fondly of Tokushima and the Setting Sons Chapter.

As they drive away, pennants rippling, Mass quietly throws up into the neatly mown grass by the temple gate. When I go to help him, offer paper tissues, water from the bottle on my bike, he waves me away, angry, afraid. For the rest of the day's ride to Temple Nineteen he will not speak to me. The incident with the akiras has affected him out of all proportion to the cause. For my part I am content with his silence; I have my own inner reaches to plumb: the seduction of power, the narrowness of my escape, a grace—the Daishi, walking with me?—that has so far permitted only the selfless use of my power while preventing the selfish, the harmful. But even selflessness is failure: I have crossed half the planet to come on this pilgrimage to break that power absolutely. The sky is crisscrossed with the contrails of many aircraft—local aerospace forces, weaving an intricate pattern of defense in the ionosphere I cannot decipher.

Our prayers in the Daishi Hall at Temple Nineteen are dry and lifeless; a computer (read secretarial) error at our hotel has assigned our room to a brace of interior designers over from Osaka for the week-long Shinto anniversary. It is the big annual download. The place is busier than Bethlehem in a census. If apologies were roof tiles we would sleep warm and dry but as they are not, we find shelter in a truckers' coffin hotel on the faded side of town. "No tattoos" says the sign behind the reception desk.

"No room at the inn," I joke but the girl on the desk doesn't have the referential baggage and Mas still isn't speaking. I am reluctant to leave the demon box in a locker in the communal changing room but the other guests in their uniform blue checkered kimonos and tabi are already politely not staring and, after the akiras, I am wary of provoking interest. The box on the third level—padded, air-conditioned, with integral videophone, radio, television, minibar (I raid the chocolate, pass, ruefully, on the Scotch), and service call button—is pleasingly womblike, if not exactly designed with people of my height in mind. I remember a bullshitting Beefeater once showing me the cell in the Tower of London called "Little Ease" that was too short, too narrow, too low to allow its occupant to stand or lie straight. Torture. I flick across television channels: sport, sport, chat show, sport, EmTeeVee, ads, ads, an old British sitcom that wasn't funny when I first saw it fifteen years ago. No Danjuro 19: *Kabukiman!* I find *le porno* but the plotless, artless slomo-ing of rounded chunks of oiled anatomy to what sounds like the Japanese idea of Harlem elevator music is deeply depressing, utterly anti-erotic.

I surface from contorted fleshtone dreams—falling asleep with the television on—wakened but not knowing what has woken me. The big rack of sleep pods shakes to the thunder of passing trucks, plumbing gurgles, air-conditioning whirs like a gray moth. A cry—more a wail—a voice begging for them not to hurt her don't hurt her please don't hurt her. Mas's voice, beyond the thin plastic wall.

Crouching on the mesh catwalk, I hammer on the coffin door until he opens. *I heard you cry out, is anything the matter, what's wrong?*

Nothing is the matter, nothing is wrong, everything is fine just fine he says but I see that his face is stone, hard stone, the face of a man who has been my friend all my adult life. Betrayed, confused, frightened, I return to my dark coffin in a far foreign country, and seek the pale comfort of memories.

Luka conceived them. Later, when she saw their true faces she would disown them but her words, her speculations, were the seed; the ten parts per thousand pisswater of the Nineteenth House pool the amniotic fluid in which conception took place.

"Jesus Joseph and Mary, a pool!" was Luka's first reaction on arriving with Masahiko; Marcus, and 'Becca to take up Ethan Ring's offer of summer hospitality in the sun. Thereafter she spent a significant part of every day stroking up and down, up and down, up and down; clear, glossy water shedding across her back, the crest of hair slicked across her shaved scalp, her brown shoulders. "Bet you never guessed I had an Esther Williams fetish. Why couldn't they have had kinships for men, and why couldn't my dad been in one? I was a deprived child, sympathy sympathy."

On the third morning that the thermometer stuck at ninety-eight, they all decided to follow Luka's example, returned to the primeval semi-aquatic state, and congregated breast-deep in the deep end around a floating tin bath full of slushy ice studded with bottles of import beer. Immersed in cool water, their talk turned to ambitions, hopes, fears, art, ideas.

"I've an idea!" Luka shouted. Bottles were deftly uncapped on the tiled pool edge, bottle caps sashayed down through the green-tinted water to form improbable constellations on the bottom. "Wrap this in a Rizla and toke it. In every piece of art or architecture or design there is an essence, a visual element that bypasses conscious discrimination and stimulates a direct psychological—even physiological—effect. Something that precedes understanding, analysis, interpretation, appreciation; that hits straight home in some deep reptile part of the brain and fires it off. Like, say, patterns of color and shape that create an overpowering impression—even a feeling—of dread, without there being any image you could specifically identify as *dreadful.*"

"Like emotional response?" asked 'Becca, floating on her back with a bottle of Becks balanced between her breasts.

"More powerful than that. More primal. Pre-emotional. Chemical."

"I'm only a mere designer, but isn't the whole point of abstract art to stimulate this kind of response?" asked Marcus.

"It strikes me that this effect can only be found in abstract art." This from Masahiko, pressing a fresh-from-the-bath beer bottle to his forehead. "Ecstasy. In representational art, or design, the strength of the image itself would drown out this ... preconscious effect."

Ethan considered the flags rattling from the mastheads of the sleek white cruisers down in the marina before speaking.

"Not necessarily. Not at all. Like I once read this book." Hoots of derision. Ethan persevered. "Like I said, I once read this book about typography, by this really famous designer from back in the eighties, nineties: Neville Brody. Neville Brody?" Shrugs. "Barbarians. Well, there's a bit I remember where he talks about a typeface being 'authoritarian.' At the time I thought, *What is this shit, how can letters on a page convey authority?* But he was right; it's exactly the same thing you're talking about, Loo."

"Call me that once more, Ethan Ring, and you're catfood."

"That the form of the letters in which a message is printed can somehow embed a subliminal meta-text?" asked Masahiko.

"I wouldn't have put it quite like that, but yes."

"You mean, like printing political pamphlets in heavy, dark sans serif type can make the reader subconsciously more susceptible to the message than if it were in an italic or script font?" 'Becca suggested.

"Conversely," said Luka brightly, "you could set the Koran in one of those ghastly 1970s fonts made up from Art Nouveau women's faces as an act of graphic subversion."

"To get back to Luka's original idea," Ethan Ring said, "does there exist, is it possible to construct, the ultimate authoritarian typeface? One in which the embedded subconscious message is so powerful that the reader has to obey whatever is written in it?"

"To hear is to obey," Marcus said.

"To see is to obey," Luka corrected. "Shut up, you guys, Ethan has something here." He was wagging a finger at unseen choirs of Muses, sucking in his lower lip, and gazing at the bottom right quadrant of heaven as he did when the creative saps were flowing in him.

"Are there, in fact, whole families of these things, out there, in there, somewhere; pure refined forms of what we have been talking about. Visual"—he caught at words—"entities that the conscious mind can't process, that slip past our powers of rationality and discrimination and stimulate direct, physical responses. Like joy, or anger, or religious ecstasy, like getting high. Or even entirely new altered states of consciousness."

"Buddhist mandalas are supposed to open the mind

to nirvana," Masahiko threw in. "Perhaps mandalas, abstract art, different styles of typography, all contain hints, diluted forms of these things Eth's talking about. The true visual entities, the pure forms, the absolute forms, await to be seen, synthesized, isolated."

" 'Lost Acres,' " 'Becca said. "An old poem by Robert Graves, I think. Didn't they teach you anything at school?"

"Wanking mostly," said Marcus. "And how to roll joints one-handed."

"Shows. 'Lost Acres' is about how small parts of the landscape disappeared due to surveying errors. I'm not exactly sure how, but bits of fields, lanes, hedgerows, woods, got folded up and never appeared on the maps. On the map, A-ville will be right next to B-town; on the ground, there could be entire geographies in between."

"Hidden realities. Bit Swords'n'Sorcery for me," Marcus said.

"Like these entities may be the lost acres of the mind, things that have been overlooked by the higher consciousness; that it can't see them, can't process them, fills in the space where they are by folding up the visual map around them, putting things on either side next to each other, like the blind spot in the eye." 'Becca again.

"Perhaps they all exist in the blind spot," Masahiko said. "Perhaps that's what the blind spot is, the part of the eye that registers these visual entities the mind can't see."

"Like the way the natural world embeds complex chaotic forms, like fractals, or the Mandelbrot set, that we find difficult to process," Ethan said.

"Maybe consciousness is nothing more than a filtering mechanism so that we can go about our daily lives without being blinded by the constant light of God," Luka said.

"Hey hey hey hey," Marcus interrupted. "This is getting the teeniest bit scary, boys and girls."

That night the marina burned. All the Nineteenth House and its neighbors in the unit turned out to watch the blaze and pass around cocktails and binoculars.

"Pure fucking apocalypse, the biggest burn since the Spanish Armada and I can't find my fucking palmcorder!" Luka screamed in frustration. Someone was wheeling out a barbecue. Up on the road behind the Nineteenth House, the car headlights were nose to tail.

"What we were saying this afternoon," Marcus confided to Ethan. "I think I know how it could be done. Expert systems sift images, locate those areas that embed this nonconscious stimulus thing, stack them to isolate common factors, and image-processing software amplifies and enhances them." Ethan was less than half listening to Marcus's evangelism, hot dogs and curled-up burgers were going round; Nikki Ring had brought out a beatbox. The flames were now throwing themselves thirty to forty meters into the hot summer night. A gasp from the assembled spectators: a gas cylinder had gone up with a scream and starburst like a rocket. Not even the Coronation fireworks had been this good.

"They reckon it's terrorists," said Masahiko, accepting something vaguely vodka-ey/orangey from one of Ethan's co-sisters. "Islamic, Zionist, Third-World Debt-defaultist, Basque, Irish."

'Becca appeared on the terrazzo with the palmcorder that she had found under a pile of Luka's dirty underwear. Luka kissed her flamboyantly and with a rebel yell was over the fence, down on the beach, and running toward the conflagration, viewfinder pressed to eye.

"You are one lucky lucky bastard, Ethan Ring," said Masahiko and for the first time Ethan Ring knew and understood and appreciated and valued what he had with Luka. He wanted then to just stand and look at her, flamelit, videoing thirteen million ecus of burning yacht but Marcus was a persistent whisper in his ear.

"Think about it, Eth. Think what you could get for a graphic image that does everything E-Base does with no side effects no addiction problem no accidental overdose; think what they would pay for a typeface that makes you obey whatever is written in it."

"Marcus, it was a joke. A joke, that's all."

"Many a true word spoken in jest, Eth."


It was beautiful. It looked like ... It looked like ... Like ...

"There's nothing there," said Ethan Ring. The thing slipped from his field of vision like a glass eel. "I don't see anything."

New term in the rainy-day city. Same faces, same places, moved up a year, October outside the computer suite windows. Masahiko had logged off tonight's installment of *Kinjiru* Cyber Les-girls. The last technician had issued the ritual admonition to switch off the lights *and nothing else* and left the room of humming monitors to the three pioneers, and the thing Marcus had found.

"You can't see anything," said Luka Casipriadin.

"Luka's right," said Marcus Cranitch. "It's the blind spot effect we talked about. It's there all right." Qwerty icons were summoned. "If I enlarge the image by a factor of ten ..."

The visual nothingness opened like a lotus blooming and engulfed them.

It was awe and it was wonder. It was beauty and it was terror. It was purity and it was judgment. It was everything and nothing, void and light, annihilation and creation. Alpha and Omega. The Primal *Fiat*. The Great I Am. It was love and truth and justice and holiness and might, everything every book, every verse, every mantra, every sutra, said it was. It was every spiritual experience, every dervish dance, every glimmer of nirvana, every shaman trance, every elevation into rapture. It was more. Vastly more.

It was the face of God. The room shook. The computer suite was filled with the sound of a rushing mighty wind. Tongues of fire seemed to dance on the heads and hands of the trinity of observers, their lips moved with ecstatic utterances in languages never before heard on the tongues of humans.

After a time that seemed like a foretaste of eternity, Luka's voice was heard. " 'My face you shall not see, for no man may see my face and live.' " Her words seemed to come through a cavernous white roar, as of angels' wings beating before the throne of God. "But we see, we fucking see, and live!"

Every word of Marcus's was a boulder of rationality pushed up the asymptotic incline of ecstasy.

"I accessed the National Gallery's datacore for religious art and icons and set the program parameters to flag me every time it came on something that corresponded to my definition of the spiritual, the numinous, the irrational. Have you any idea how many Madonna and Childs I had to look at before I got a big enough sample? It took the machine three days to collate and render the samples I stored, another overnight fifteen-hour run to enhance the image."

"And what came out in the end is something that stimulates the human facility for religious ecstasy," Ethan said, his words slipping, sliding into the light-filled voice of God.

"You got it. All those icons, all those mandalas and Sanskrit mantras and illuminated Celtic manuscripts, they're just reflections, hints, memories, explorations. This is the true glory."

And the transfiguration was gone. The glory lifted. God's face turned away. Only painful afterimages remained and a piercing sense of Paradise Lost. Luka's hand moved from the off switch.

"We aren't supposed to see these things. God hides his face for a reason. Humankind cannot bear too much divinity."

"Secrets too terrible for Mankind to know?" Marcus's scorn flayed. "Old sci-fi hokum. This is just the start. If there's one, there've got to be others. And I'm going to find them."

Luka shook her head.

"Dump it, Marcus. Erase it, smash it, get rid of it. It's dangerous. It'll burn you. It'll destroy you. I promise."


Shingon and the Art of Mountain Bike Maintenance. I am up before dawn. It is a good time, the new hours, the fresh hours; the best time. Things are clearer. The air is crisp, cold, clean, the sky a prefaded shrink-fit denim blue deepening over the zenith to fresh, prewash indigo. The moon has been down for an hour. I sit on the curb dwarfed by the monolithic masses of trucks pulled in for the night at the coffin hotel, working patiently, steadily. When your safety depends on diligence, you do not rush your repairs. There is much value in tinkering with bicycles. As much as in riding bicycles, there is a state one enters where *I* and *you* cease to matter, where subject and object are abolished, where you and it become one thing, one unity, one awareness. True cyborg: man/machine fusion.

As I thought, the seatings for the thumb-shifts have worked loose. I tighten them with a small screwdriver from my toolkit, lubricate with a squirt or two of oil from the aerosol spray I carry in my belt pouch, and the sun comes over the roof tiles of Temple Nineteen on its hillside.

A hand touches my shoulder.

Mas. Bike ready. Bags packed. Kitted up.

"Just fixing the index system," I say. "It kept slipping out of gear yesterday." He nods, slides his wraparound shades beneath the dome of his henro hat and we are off, running down through the streets with the town waking up around us. Shops roll up their steel shutters; children hurry to school, multicolored backpacks swaying; delivery vans hum and purr through streets decorated with bunting and lanterns and banners for the Shinto festival. I share their sense of jubilee; of being on holiday, with one's own agendas and destinations while elsewhere the world grinds on in the mundanities of work/eat/TV/sleep/work/eat/TV/sleep.

This stretch of henro path, from Temple Nineteen to Temple Twenty-three, is dense with connections to the life of the Daishi. The next valley over from Twenty contains the temple's inmost sanctuary, a deep cave at the head of a narrow canyon where the saint meditated. Perhaps next pilgrimage. At Temple Twenty-one, atop

Mount Tairyu—we must leave the bikes, and scramble up on foot—the Daishi attempted to invoke his guardian deity, Kokuzo, in a month-long ritual. No priest now—none are prepared to make the daily climb—but the diskperson guides from the yencard dispenser relish in the esoteric detail of the Daishi's ritual: chanting the Mantra of Light one million times, painting the moon on a pure white sheet, and on the moon an image of Kokuzo, and on the image of Kokuzo a crown, and on the crown forty Buddhas, and in the palm of each Buddha an open lotus, and in each lotus a pearl emitting yellow rays ...

"And so ad infinitum," I comment.

It was not on the mountaintop that Kobo Daishi attained enlightenment, but in a sea cave at the eastern tip of the Muroto peninsula. And it is toward Cape Muroto, toward the sea, that we journey through whispering groves of bamboo—always, to me, a deeply spiritual sound, the voice of the Buddha of the valley. I can smell the ocean now beyond the hills where Temple Twenty-two lies hidden like a pearl in a lotus. As ever, it fills me with its divine discontent. Sea changes. Mas has not spoken to me, but I sense that his spiritual tide is on the turn. Our silence is the silence of two friends who do not need words to express their closeness. We have passed the barrier gate.

The henro path from Twenty-two to Twenty-three has been overlain with blacktop and is now the pawing ground of monstrous, fast-moving juggernauts. Our maps mark an alternative coastal route: a good-riding switchback of a path with sheer forested hills on one side and the serene blue Pacific on the other. Nirvana between the mountains and the sea. We cross a rocky headland and before us is a curving beach of white sand.

At the end of it, the town of Hiyasa and the many-colored steeple of Temple Twenty-three's pagoda.

I yell to Mas; he is as willing as I to pause awhile in this beautiful place. The water is cold; almost a physical shock. Air says late May, ocean says early March. I yell and flap and flubber enough to convince my long-cherished ambition to swim in every major ocean, then come running out, flicking long ropes of droplets from my hair. Mas waits beneath the outstretched branch of an ancient pine, like a blessing hand, drawing with light, fluid strokes of a brush pen. Turtles.

It's good to see him drawing again.

"Every spring, about this time, they come to lay their eggs," he says. "Every year, for millions of years, something calls them back to this beach to lay their eggs by the full moon. Long before we were, they came; long after we are gone, all of us, and all our plans and ambitions, they will return still.

"I take great reassurance from that."

He signs and dates the drawing in his sketchbook, titles it *Turtle Beach, Temple Twenty-three, Moon's Third Quarter: Namu Daishi Henjo Kongo.*

After a time, Masahiko speaks again.

"I remember, years ago, we talked. That summer we all came down to your place, we talked about graphic entities that stimulated direct physical responses. A typeface that embedded subconscious images so that the reader would find it impossible to resist what the message said."

"I remember that conversation."

"You did it, didn't you?"

My gloved fists clench instinctively. To relax them takes a mighty effort of will.

"Tell me, Ethan."

"Yes. We did. Yes."

"The Morikawa girl."

"Healing is one of them. Laughter too. Tears. Ecstasy. Fear. Pain. Many many more. We named them after angels, the Sefirahs, but they deceived us."

Mas laughs, bitter and theatrical; a kabuki laugh. "All this time, and I never knew I was traveling in the company of Danjuro 19 himself."

"I'm no superhero, Mas. There are no superheroes, there is no James Bond; life isn't *anime*."

"Those akiras." The word is like vomit to him. "You could have—I don't know—frightened them, blinded them." An unsuspected tight, clenched anger in Mas explodes. "Burned out their fucking brains."

"I didn't need to. You heard them say Kabukiman was always the friend of true akiras. They thought you were God."

"I didn't ask them to be Kabukiman freaks. I didn't ask to be God; I didn't ask for their adulation and hero worship and telling me how Danjuro stands for everything that is holy to them when everything they stand for, everything they are, makes me sick; sick, Ethan, like cancer in my stomach, and angry, and afraid; sick, angry, and afraid." He is silent, tight, clenched within himself so long I think he has nothing more to say. It is only the pause for a deeper pain to percolate through the sands of the spirit.

"We were going to get married. She was a PR manager for my Tokyo distributors. I met her at the Free Queensland *Kabukiman!* launch. I loved her. Like that." Five fingers snap, like a trap closing. "It can happen." I know. "More often than people think." I know that too, Masahiko.

Out on the ocean, million-ton ore carriers are

moving ponderously between probabilities of tropical storms. Beyond them, a low dark smear is an offshore arcology burning, staining the horizon with oily smoke. Down the beach toward the town, two kids are throwing sticks for a woolly dog.

"She moved in with me after three days. She was like that, she would do things because she felt like doing them. She had this bobtail cat: a *mi-ke*, the rarest kind, blind in one eye. It would sit in the window and look down at the street. Sometimes it would bat at the people it saw moving down there. It thought they were insects. Didn't have 3-D vision, you see. I had to work a lot at night—got into bad ways at art college, you remember, when I had to steal computer time to work on *Kinjiru* Cyber Les-girls, that's where Kabukiman started, Danjuro had a walk-on part. She would bring me endless cups of coffee. She made the only perfect coffee. She measured it, you see. Funny; the big things fade, her face, her body; it's the small things that remain; cats, coffee. She used to play volleyball up on the roof, in those tight, cute shorts they wear, and kneeguards and elbow pads. Kneeguards, elbow pads, and shorts, they remain floating in space. I can't see her anymore. Isn't that strange? I loved to watch her running, jumping, shouting, totally unself-conscious. She was beautiful, I loved her.

"They killed her."

An aged aged couple comes poking along the tideline with sticks, turning over wrack, driftwood, looking for treasures floated from mythic California. An aircraft makes a long, slow left turn, beginning its descent toward the Tokyo Bay hypurbation.

"That stupid car. It was one of the first of the new model Daihatsu 4×4s, when the biomotors were being introduced and it was a real status symbol to have one. She could be very stupid that way, about things like status. Very vain, sometimes. 'Give it up,' I told her. 'It's only a damn car, let the akiras have it.' She sat there with both hands on the wheel with that piss-on-you look I knew so well, the one she'd turn on me when I did something she didn't approve of, and everyone was shouting, all there was was shouting and the sound of police sirens approaching and she said to me, 'Get in we're going' and—you know the way it happens in films when it all goes slow motion and you think reality is nothing like that, but it's true—it was like I saw it all in slow motion: the Boss taking one step back to get a clear shot, the way the machine-pistol jerked in his hand as he emptied the magazine into her, the way it opened her up, like a fish—can you believe it, that was what I thought, like a fileted bonito, the sound the last cartridge case made as it hit the concrete, the blare of the horn as she fell against it and how suddenly it stopped when they pulled her onto the street, how much blood there was, an amazing amount of blood, I didn't think there could be so much blood in one body ... Funny, isn't it? The one thing I can't remember is the sound of the firing. They took the car. Incredible, she was still alive when the ambulance came. She didn't make it to the hospital. They got the akiras, you know. Chiba Security put the heads on display at the main district shrine.

"She was beautiful. I loved her. They killed her. Ethan, what is happening to my country? What's gone wrong?"

He cries unashamedly. Cold and wet, I fold him in my arms, offer him comfort. The aged aged couple pass by and murmur fondly to each other, misunderstanding.

The tide advances up the beach. The big ships vanish one by one below the horizon. The edge of night approaches low across the ocean. Growing chill, I pull on shirt, zip-up jacket, track bottoms. I think about the turtles moving out there under many, many fathoms of water. I think about the burning arcologies.

Malkhut: who sees the face of angels, *obeys*.

Yesod: Empire of the senses, domain of limitless pleasure.

Hod: glory: full frontal God.

Nezah: pain: emotional anguish, spiritual torment, physical agony, existential angst.

Tiferet: healing and wholeness.

Gevurah: terror. Pure. Raw. Absolute. Terror.

Hesed: arousal to orgasm in under three seconds.

Binah: the fracter that annihilates the sense of time the creator of order.

Hokhmah: forgetting. Utterly, instantly, irrevocably.

It was as if that one glimpse of the face of God had set in motion a wave of crystallization that precipitated entire choirs and chapters of visual entities. Every night, at the Hour of Harassed Cleaners, perceptual pioneers Cranitch and Ring would watch the un-images—*fracters*, Ethan Ring's coinage—unfold from their blind spots into things that sent them into paroxysms of laughter or hysterical weeping or plunged them into suicidal depression or took them to highs that the designers of the new mass-market synthetics could only hope for in wet dreams or left them paralyzed, immobile, dropped into stasis by a display that annihilated their sense of time until the fail-safe timer blanked the display and released them. Marcus, having digested The Illuminati during his teenage paranoia years, suggested naming them after the ten Sefirot of the Hebrew Cabala.

Luka now only visited the C.A.D. suite to issue warnings to Ethan. Marcus she must have thought beyond hope of salvation. Her visits to the sixth floor and the mayhem of Design Communications decreased correspondingly. She no longer came knocking on his downstairs door. It was months since she had slept with him, or stolen his shopping. Ethan stopped her on the stairs one Thursday evening in the hope that a confrontation might cause her to relent.

"Why? Close encounter between two Trans-Atlantics this morning?"

"A smart mouth isn't you, Eth. Okay. Why. You've been lucky so far, what happens one day you're gawking at the screen and up comes something that induces psychotic rage? Or total amnesia? How about schizophrenia, how about epilepsy, or suicidal depression, or worse? It frightens me. There. That's it out in the open. Luka Casipriadin, that girl who isn't afraid of nothing? This scares her. Just because I got this natty Mohawk doesn't make me a cyberpunk ice-queen. This. Scares. Me. Fuckless. It scares me fuckless because I love you, Ethan Ring, and you're too fucking stupid to realize it."

Ethan reported the conversation, minus the last eighteen words verbatim.

"*Worse,*" Marcus mused. Their experiments had now taken them into the realm of the Diabolicals, subfracters—now numbering over one hundred—evolved from permutation of the Sefirah program parameters. "Gives you that cold prickle right down in your balls, doesn't it, Eth? Like when you know you're going to get laid. She always could put her finger right on it. There is bigger game out there waiting for us. The biggest game. Epilepsy, amnesia, psychosis, sure. But sometime you got to put it all on the line for the big one. Live on the edge. Kiss the razor. Every explorer knows he's taking a risk. That's what we are, Eth; mental explorers, psychonauts, going deep in the darkest places of the mind."

"One hundred percent pure rockist macho bullshit," said Ethan Ring. "You'll be asking me to sniff your armpits next."

"You going to let Luka Casipriadin tell you what's game and what's not?"

Two fistfuls of black denim shirt. Face ten centimeters from face. The closest range of social interaction: lovemaking range, violent anger range. Taste-my-breath distance.

"You are within *this* of having your face pushed through that screen, Marcus Cranitch."

Illuminatus. Ethan Ring saw the unsuspected depths of anger within him, the fear he had made appear on Marcus's face, and was afraid. It was as if one of his mothers had sat him down and told him, quietly, fearfully, of some hitherto unmentioned congenital defect: schizophrenia, hemophilia, AIDS, lycanthropy. Ethan Ring, his life, his history, were a pretense, a robing and masking of the glass-hearted monster that was the true Ethan Ring. For an instant—brief but real—he had been filled with a hot, unclean excitement at the image of Marcus's face smashing the curved glass of the monitor into cubes and crumbs. He fled the computer suite. He fled the university and everything to do with it. He hid for three days behind his artless posters and CDs and scraps of unsuccessful projects. Then he could no longer bear to look at the face of his anger and went to ask forgiveness. There was one light in the darkened, murmuring computer suite.

"Marcus.

"Marcus, I'm sorry. I just sometimes go kind of mad, you know?

"I've come to apologize, Marcus.

"Say something Marcus, don't make me feel worse than I do now.

"Marcus? You okay?

"Marcus!"

The figure on the floor, lit blue by the light of the screen, lay supine, head tilted back, repeatedly slamming the rear of its skull against the cigarette-burned floor tiles. Arms and legs thrashed, the body convulsed epileptically. Tears of blood trickled from each eye, down the cheeks, onto the floor.

"Christ, Marcus!" Ethan Ring came around the desk to touch, to help, to do something, anything, *anything*. And the thing in the blue screen reached out and smashed him against the wall.


Once, when Ethan Ring was a boy, he had given himself a severe electric shock playing with an old television.

Once Ethan Ring caught some mutant strain of influenza that sent his temperature to 103 and hallucinated he was climbing the concrete and glass face of an infinite office block, up and up and up and up and up.

Once, Nikki Ring's old Vauxhall Nova with Ethan-at-seven in the backseat had been sideswiped at a dark country crossing by something that did not stop and it had been spun three times around before Ethan Ring came to looking at a billboard proclaiming "All Have Sinned and Fallen Short of the Glory of God."

Once, Ethan Ring, walking merrily mellow back to his flat, had been set upon by two young white men in designer sportswear who headbutted him, kicked him in the small of the back, and relieved him of eighty ecus and a take-away curry.

The thing in the screen was all those. The thing in the screen was more. It was *shock*. Toxic karmic physical spiritual emotional culture techno socio cold turkey pure total utter: shock.

His heart skipped and misfired. His breath fluttered. His head screamed *migraine* at him. His hands, his arms, his legs, would not obey him but thrashed spastically. Urgent nausea pressed at the base of his gullet. He opened his eyes. The thing in the screen leapt out of his peripheral vision and slammed his brain against the inside of his skull. He waited forever hiding inside his skull until proprioception told him his body would now do what he told it. Eyes closed, he groped across the floor. He swore at his hands *stop shaking, stop fucking shaking*. His eyes flickered at the touch of soft, spasming flesh. No. No. Medusa's sister, basilisk's brother. To look upon their faces was to die. Fingers climbed the desk leg, crossed the desktop, found the *off* switch, and pushed it. Almost, he opened his eyes. Almost. Marcus could have printed out a hardcopy. Fingers felt their way to the printer, delved into its nooks and crevices. Nothing. He opened his eyes. The disk. The fracter disk. He ejected it from the drive. It burned his hand like an ingot of white iron. Taking the elevator to the front door was eternal torment.

"If you boys spent as much time on your projects as

you did in the Union bar ..." admonished the door-
man, well used to student excess.

"An ambulance!" Ethan Ring screamed. "Call a
fucking ambulance!"

The last of the ten Sefirot was enthroned.

Keter: the Void. *Annihilation.*


There is to be a Fire Ceremony tonight at Temple
Twenty-four. All are welcome, Priest Tsunoda tells us.
He is a small, vigorous man of great charm and cha-
risma; a retired cram-school teacher in Beloved School-
master tradition of Bette Davis, Robert Donat, Robin
Williams. The stories that roost around this isolated
cluster of three Temples at the tip of the Muroto Peninsula whisper that he could have been a Nobel laureate
in his chosen field of mathematics, but he renounced
worldly fame and the praises of men to devote his life
to what he called "subversion through education": ke-
babing the Japanese sacred cow of exam-cram-4-job-4-
life-in-the-Company on the thin, dangerous skewer of
learning for learning's sake. School governors, PTAs, local politicians, villified him. His students deified him.
Bertrand Russell's quotable: "How good it is to know
things!" had been painted above his chalkboard. It followed him to Temple Twenty-four with only one
change: the addition of the prefix "un" to the penulti-
mate word of the motto.

"One third of your life to learn things, and the rest
of it to unlearn all the rubbish they cram into you," he
says as he shows us to our neat, scrupulously clean
room, scented with sandalwood, lavender, and the sea.
"Quality: to know what is good, what is not good, and
why: that was what I was trying to teach. If even a

handful learned that, I can pass from this world content."

Cape Muroto is a sixty-mile shark's-tooth hooked into the skin of the Western Pacific Basin. Its northern face is a forbidding scarp of sheer black cliff, its southern a grand sweep of sandy bays and headlands terminating in Cape Ashizuri two hundred kilometers to the south. *Enola Gay* used Moroto as a landmark en route from Tinian Island to her two minutes of fame over Hiroshima. To the henro, it marked in no uncertain terms the arrival of the hardships of Tosa Prefecture.

> *Tosa is the Devil's country,*
> *No hospitality there, you may be sure.*

complained a sixteenth-century henro. The names may have changed—it's Kōchi Prefecture now—but the song remains the same.

We were ten kilometers out on the main road east out of Hiyasa—not a route we would have chosen but the rough coastal terrain made beach riding impossible—when we hit the checkpoint. We came on it unawares, blindsided by a line of trucks. Glimpsing uniforms and flashing blue lights between the walls of traffic, we imagined an RTA. Only at the head of the queue did we see our mistake. Two armored personnel carriers—ex-military—were parked across the highway; on their flanks, on the helmets and shoulders of the armored men checking the vehicles through one by one was a symbol of an eagle clutching crossed lightning bolts in its talons and the name: Tosa Securities Incorporated.

They were the ones who had caused Mr. Morikawa's death at Temple Twelve. We were entering the heart of their empire.

"Purging undesirable elements, they tell you," the driver of a pickup told us. He was transporting a load of young trees with their roots wrapped in wet sacking. "My ass. It's good old medieval transit tax."

A white-helmeted, white-gloved private policeman beckoned us forward, polite, but eternally a policeman. Our security transit passes—supposedly good for all the private forces on the pilgrimage route—henro albums, and my European passport were examined minutely, then taken for further examination by an unseen officer inside one of the troop transports. I found it a thoroughly disagreeable sensation, to have one's identity, one's right to move and be, taken away, to be so vulnerable. After ten minutes our papers were returned stamped with transit permits and thirty-day policy cover-notes for which we were required to part with thirty thousand yen each.

At least you could tell Long John Silver by the parrot on his shoulder. I could not rid myself of the impression that my documents had been digitally scanned. They smelled vaguely ... electronic, like fresh photocopies, or faxes. Everything in order, the policeman welcomed us to Kōchi Prefecture, advised us to stick wherever possible to the signposted Approved Tourist Route as "Antisocial Elements" were still active and he could not guarantee that our policy would fully cover us if we wandered off the proper way. He politely bowed us through. Dodgy cover or not, we were seldom so glad to find an opportunity to turn off the Approved Tourist Route onto the old henro path.

The Way, through coastal towns, along fearsome cliff paths, was terrifying and thrilling. The eighty-kilometer stretch between Twenty-three and Twenty-four—to us, only a strenuous day's ride—with few towns and less alms persuaded many to rethink their calling to the pilgrim life. One chronicler of the pilgrimage comments that Awa, the prefecture behind us, was famed for its perfection of the art of the ballad-drama. Tosa bred fighting dogs. On the coast road stand stone images of Jizo, protector of children, living gateway between worlds, rescuer of the perishing from the torments of hell. The images all look out to sea, watching over the souls of sailors, fishermen, and all who go down to the sea in ships. Hard land. Stern spirits.

Though it is late, and we are tired, Priest Tsunoda advises us to visit the sea caves while there is still light. Tucked between the roots of a subtropical banyan, the wave-cut caves are wide, low, dry, intricately intersecting with each other. This is the place where the Daishi at last achieved enlightenment as the morning star, the avatar of Kokuzo, rose out of Yakushi's Pure World in the East. Pilgrims have built cairns of flat sea-washed stones in commemoration of his achievement, as pilgrims will. The sound of the sea is oddly muted, the air moves in odd vortices through the interlinked caves, but try as I might I cannot find in myself any of that ancient spirit of ecstasy and tranquillity. All long since carried away with the flotsam on the flooding tide. The light is fading fast now, shadows fusing and melting into greater darknesses. I lift a stone to place it on a cairn. In the dark recesses of the grotto a shadow moves.

My right hand moves toward the cuff of my left glove.

"Sorry to have alarmed you, brother henro," a refined male voice says. There is a strange, arthropodal clicking. Something moves in the shadows, steps toward us on too many feet. Far too many feet. Half man, half ... "Please, place your stone," the hemi-human says. "Permit me to introduce myself. Mr. Spider at your service."

As he clicks and hums his way over the rocks he tells us the story of his last two incarnations on his way to enlightenment. He first was as Kiyoshi Ueno, number one salesperson of the IkoIko Zipper Company; then came his head-to-head encounter one Tuesday night with a ghost-driver in the fast lane of the West Bay Elevated SkyWay. Closing velocity: two hundred kph; range: fifty meters; the ghost-driver chickened, lost it, and flipped across three lanes inbound to fireball out among Korean guest-workers' allotments. IkoIko Zipper Salesperson of the Year impacted with the central crash barrier and was removed to the Chiba District Trauma Center sustaining multiple fractures to fifty percent of his skeleton. After four months immobilized in a steel frame, only his spinal cord in the region of vertebrae twelve and thirteen remained unrepaired and, his doctors gently convinced him, unrepairable. At some point in those four months fixed to the corners of the metal frame the life that was Kiyoshi Ueno died and, while the attention of the medical robots was turned elsewhere, was reborn as Mr. Spider.

The mobility unit fits around the waist and supports his body in a plastic cradle. Six biomotor legs carry him across the surface of the planet; strong, tireless, but to my unenlightened eyes disturbing: synthetic muscle hooked onto metal limbs by neuroplastic sinews. At his invitation we examine the synaptic interfacers drilled into the back of his neck, the rainbow swathes of datacore. He proudly points out the corporate ident stickers plastered over every available surface of his walker. Similar logos adorn his henro hat and robe. His stole is sponsored by the Sea of Tranquillity Holistic Drinks Company, his staff by Sony. His henro bell, made for him by one of the last Living Treasures, the irreplaceable master craftspersons of Japan, rings continuously as he moves with a deep, ocean-clear voice, oddly tranquil for such restlessness.

"The Daishi gave me back my gift of mobility so that I might use it not for myself, as I did when I was Kiyoshi Ueno, but for others," he says. Since leaving rehab he has raised money for just causes by the simple—for some—act of walking. The Tokaido first, then the pilgrimage of the thirty-three temples of Kannon that cross the spine of Honshu from sea to shining sea. After that climbing Mount Koya to the Shingon capital on its summit, and going straight on to complete the miniature circular pilgrimage of temples on Shodo Island in the Inland Sea. These, he says, were merely preparations for this his heart's desire, the great Shikoku pilgrimage. Twenty major companies are sponsoring him or have donated funds to enable him to make the trip; the number of individuals runs into the hundreds. A Tokyo media-news company are payrolling him for progress reports; he faxes them in as regularly as the humbler pace of a foot pilgrim will permit. With the money he hopes to alleviate the suffering of children worldwide.

"We are the most terrible of species," he says. "Only praying mantises hate and mistreat their offspring more."

True holiness, I suppose, is like true humility. The one who claims to possess it is the furthest from it. Mr.

Spider would be deeply shocked if he were told he was a true *hijiri*.

After dinner, Mas apologizes and slips out to make a lengthy 'phone call. Mr. Spider and I take tea and oranges and he tells me his pilgrim's tales. May he mention us in his next report? Priest Tsunoda has said he may use the temple fax. I would deem it an honor, I tell him, and it is not mere polite formalism. Time spent in the company of remarkable men is time well spent.

We go up to the Fire Ceremony, where we are joined by two others, young women, one of them heavily pregnant. We kneel, we five, before the central image of the Buddha, exquisitely crafted, as things must be in Shingon, the two young women, Mas, me, Mr. Spider, his metal legs folded beneath him like some cyborg centaur in repose.

One hundred and eight sticks of fragrant wood for the hundred and eight illusions of man.

Fire leaps in the stone basin on the altar, chases strange shadows from the recesses of the Daishi Hall.

The gong is struck. The bells rung. The mantras chanted. The prayers recited.

One by one, the hundred and eight sticks—the delusions of the material world, the hardships of the spiritual way, the ·sins of man's condition—are fed to the flames.

Doves rustle their rice-paper wings under the hammerbeams of the roof.

Fragrant leaves, incenses, oils, are cast upon the fire. Shadows move upon the priest's face, like uneaten sins driven from the lips and nostrils by the influx of penetrating light.

In all the world, there are only two sounds. The voice of Priest Tsunoda intoning the prayers. The heavy thump of the surf—more felt than heard—upon the rocks beneath Temple Twenty-three. At times those two sounds flow into one sound, one universal ocean-voice. The lanterns move in the warm night wind, the shadows shift. And the sense of the numinous that had eluded me in the sea caves takes me up.

Of the time spent in that altered state of consciousness called divine ecstasy no one can speak for it transcends thought, self, language, logic. Any statement that may be made about it falls so far short of the truth of the experience as to be at best worthless, at worst misleading. Pure being. Well the medieval mystics named it the Cloud of Unknowing.

The flames gutter low. The chant ends. Beater strikes gong. The spirits are dispelled. Our sins, our weaknesses, our failures and false desires are burned to nothing. Priest Tsunoda indicates for us to draw near and rub the ashes onto whatever part of us is in need of grace. The second young woman rubs her pregnant friend's belly. The pregnant woman rubs ash onto her friend's lips, breasts, and loins. Mr. Spider rubs ash into his breast. "Keep my spirit pure, Lord Daishi," he whispers. "Keep my purposes holy." His bell whispers in reply. I lift the soft gray ash onto my fingers and rub a little carefully into the synthetic plastic palm of each hand. Mas watches me, takes ash from the firebowl, rubs it into his heart and his head.

My wooden room is too full of the sound of the sea for sleep, the moon too bright, and I fear Mas's voice crying out beyond the shoji door in a sleep through which the akiras run with banners and blades in their fists, cutting long, slow-healing gashes along the folds of his brain. I fear it because there are things in my demon box that could end his nightmares, end them as if they had never been, and I fear them more. I fear the seduction of my power. Outside in the night the temple is still, dark, the air warm, troubled only the dim ionospheric rumble of aerospacers, the trans-horizon grumble of bulk carrier engines. I walk out along the cliff edge. The broken, moonlit ocean below is an almost sexual enticement. Heights have always held an unclean fascination for me, heights over dark water most of all. When I found Luka that time in San Francisco she had invited me to join her in a long-anticipated ambition to walk the Golden Gate Bridge. ("Not run, not jog, not power-walk, not street-hike, just per-am-bu-late, Eth.") We stopped where the sweeps of cable meet to watch the radio masts and satellite dishes of a Trans-Pacific freighter pass beneath (perhaps indeed the same one I hear tonight, out on the dark ocean) and I had confessed.

"Would it shock you if I said part of me wants to climb up on the rail and jump off?"

"Born with the moon in Cancer, under the sign of two transpolars," she had said. "Self-destruction shot through you like lightning."

How easy—how appealing—to fetch my bicycle and ride off into Kannon's Pure Land in the South. I can imagine the wheels leaving the neat turf of the cliff edge. I can imagine man and machine falling together; I can anticipate the skill that will be necessary to keep us one unity, manmachine. What I cannot imagine is the impact of the moonlit, wave-washed rock.

When the voice speaks, it is as if the Daishi himself has interrupted my thoughts.

"The wounded and the maimed, so?" Mr. Spider is night-silent on his arthropod legs. "Some places are naturally more conducive to it than others. Waterfalls. Lakes. Woodland clearings. Some gardens. High places, of course. Some places can move to suicide people who would never consider killing themselves ordinarily. Think much about it, son? Nothing to be ashamed of. I do. Every day. Every day, son. Look at me, son. Look at me, what do you see? A brave man struggling against terrible disability? A hero? A saint? I'll tell you what I see. I see a travesty. A Tinkertoy man. An impotent, sterile thing kept in existence by the mercilessness of modern medicine. A man who is dead already. Dead already. Every time I look in the mirror, son, I look at death. Death in a bottle, death at the end of a rope, death under the wheels of a fast train, death at the foot of this cliff. I look, and I look, and death looks back and I see that there is something more ludicrous and disfigured and hideous and sterile and impotent than myself, and its name is death. By such small disclosures, we go on. We go on, son."

"You're a braver man than you admit, father."

"Or the greatest coward you are ever likely to meet, son."

"The greatest coward is the man who refuses to do good because of the hurt it may cause him, father. The man who fears to do good because it might cause evil."

"That depends if the man truly has power to do good, son, or is merely made impotent by guilt."

"This man has power to do good beyond your conception of power."

Mr. Spider raises his head, as if he knows the scent of a soul.

"And therefore evil."

"The reason he has come on this pilgrimage is to escape from great evil that lies in his past."

"Escape, son, may not be the way," says Mr. Spider. "It would be reassuring if everything was finally reducible to Light versus Darkness, Order versus Chaos, Good versus Evil. However, life is not pulp fantasy. If the Way were easy, what virtue would there be in following it? The teaching of the Daishi is that the Way does not lie in escape, or even in defeating. The answer to abuse is not disuse, but in the learning of right use, surely."

"I was afraid you would say that."

"So was I," says Mr. Spider.

"The Christians say all spiritual life is one beggar showing another beggar where to find bread," I say. Mr. Spider nods.

"The Daishi wrote a poem in this place," he says. He admits he has no reciting voice—it sounds like a cracked bamboo flute—but the words are strong in themselves.

> "Muroto:
> Though day in, day out,
> Waves crash, winds roar,
> Yet, still,
> The voice of the Buddha is heard."

"The Buddha of Medical Mercilessness?" I ask.

"The Buddha of the Chicken Gate?" He smiles. "I rode Space Mountain twenty-six times, in another incarnation, son." His six legs carry him carefully back along the cliff edge to the huddled dark geometries of the temple. "Sleep well, kid," he calls after me. After a time with the waves and the wind, I follow.

"Mas." I do not like to wake him from such a pure and untroubled sleep, but if I linger, my resolution will falter. "Mas." The moon is high behind me; silver light on a paper wall. I feel like a figure from poetry. "Mas."

"Ethan?"

"Healing. Laughter. Tears. Ecstasy. Fear. Pain. And forgetting. I didn't mention it, yesterday at Turtle Beach, the forgetting. I was afraid."

"Afraid of what?"

"Afraid of what you might ask me."

"To make me forget."

A subtropical moth has been trapped by the image of the moon on the shoji.

"It would be complete. It would be as if she had never existed. Is that what you want, for her to be gone from your life forever?"

"Ethan, she is gone from my life forever. I don't want to forget, I just want it to stop hurting. Can you do that?"

"There is no one fracter that can take away the hurt and leave the memory. I have one that can make you live it again, as if you were there in person; what you do with that chance to live it again is up to you."

"Ethan . . ." He grips my arm. His fingers are shapely, aesthetic.

"I'll go with you as far as I can. I have a fracter that will make sure it is never more than you can handle."

"Ethan, I can't go on the way I am."

"Then close your eyes," I tell Mas. "Don't look at me until I tell you."

The batteries in the demon box are low; two drops of syrup restore them to life. The fracters I require are low order; demons-minor, so familiar to me I have become almost immune to them: *La Serenissima* and *Mneme*. On the pine dressing table is a folded lacquered fan. I open it, peel the backings from the fracters' adhesive tabs. *La Serenissima* I place on the picture of quarreling magpies in the branches of a mountain pine; *Mneme* on the obverse, the file of happy smiling pilgrims wending down one mountain, up the next. I kneel before Masahiko, the fan open on my thighs, *La Serenissima* uppermost.

"Look now."

The breath goes out of him in a long, low sigh.

"What is it?"

"Marcus called it *La Serenissima*," I say. "Avatar of peace and tranquillity, serenity and calm. It stimulates the brain to produce endorphins, natural opiates." Mas nods slowly. His pupils are so widely dilated I imagine I can see the image of the moon contained there, whole, entire in each.

I turn the fan over in my lap.

"Mas," I say. "Remember the night she died."

Shadows cross his face, shadows from within. A movement of the moth on the paper wall, when I look back, every trace of the artificial peace of the Serenity fracter is wiped away. Only terror, helplessness, anger. Through the memory fracter, he is standing in that alley with the yellow streetlight gleaming from the polished plastic of the Daihatsu 4×4.

"Tell me, Mas."

"I'm standing shouting. I can't do anything but shout. What use is shouting? Why don't I do something? Why don't you do something? Why are you sitting there with that stupid, stupid, stupid look on your face?" It is not me he is shouting at; he cannot even see me, only the street, the night, *her*. "Don't you know that isn't going to do anything, anything but get you killed?"

"Go back," I order. "Back. How do you come to be in this street, at this time?"

A moment of *La Serenissima.*

"The basho. I forgot; it's the big sumo play-off tonight. The police have the stadium cordoned off, there are detours posted. The cars are tailed way back for several blocks. Don't bounce your hands on the horn. 'Come on come on hurry up get a move on'; look, it won't make it clear any faster. It'll clear in its own time. They'll still be around when we get there. You always were an impatient driver."

"You are not to blame," I say for the first time. "It's all right to be angry with her. She wasn't perfect, nobody's perfect. Dying hasn't made her perfect. Dying doesn't make any of us perfect. The dead can be stupid. The dead can be arrogant and impatient. You are allowed to be angry with them. You are allowed to hate them."

Mas is trembling but I do not turn the fan *La Serenissima* face outward. Not yet.

"Go back," I say. He goes back.

"Hey! I remember a way around; not exactly a shortcut, more of a long-cut, but quicker than this. I grew up near here, I should know. Anything to get her to this party, though there are reports on the radio: trouble next zone over. The security forces are trying to close down some akira chapter. I never thought they would try to break out."

Memory to tranquillity. The harmonies and rhythms of the fracter touch my peripheral vision as an almost landscapelike serenity.

"Even if you suggested the detour; even if you heard the news and thought there might be danger, still, you are not to blame," I say. And it is the second time.

"Somebody has to be to blame."

"You?"

"Who else could it be, Ethan?"

"Her. She heard the radio reports too. She decided to take the detour. Why, Mas? Where was it she was so determined to get to? Why was she so impatient?"

*Mneme* now, and Mas's face is clawed by guilt.

"Why did you want to go to the party, why did I have to agree to go with you? It would be the same thing it always is, the same faces saying the same polite things, no one ever telling me what they really think, about me, about my work. Let's give it a miss, go see a movie, go out and eat, go shopping. 'There'll be People there,' you say. 'People, from Companies. They're always headhunting, that's what these parties are really for: headhunting expeditions.' There will be Sony-Virgin-Columbia PR daimyos there with pockets full of contracts, and you'll be damned if you're going to miss out on them. You're always dreaming of this mythic, golden California. Well, maybe I don't have any ambition, maybe I'm content to be what I am, doing what I do. You get so angry when I don't do what you want. Well this time you aren't going to let my pathetic little shynesses and reclusivenesses stop you from going after what you want. Not this time."

"Would she have gone without you?"

"You're stalking up and down, up and down the hall in your party heels; it's so short you can only take three steps from end to end: click click click turn click click click turn . . ."

"Would she have gone without you?"

"Yes!" he shouted. "Yes. You would have gone. I asked you to wait five minutes while I got ready. Yes!"

"She would have gone to the party, taken the detour, ignored the warnings, run into the akiras, without you?"

"Yes," he says. "Yes. Yes!"

"You are not guilty," I say. "You are not to blame." I bring my right hand up before Mas's face. No glove. No spray-flesh. Naked. I open my fingers. *"Believe me."*

Tattooed in the palm of my right hand is the image of Malkhut, that Sefirah fracter that whoever sees it, obeys.

"Believe me." Mas's pupils dilate as the quasi-fractal shatter of images slips up his optic nerves, around the curves and folds of his visual cortex, past all logic and rationality and consciousness, into the dark, preconscious fist of the medulla where sentience first sparked out of pure animal *being* three and a half million years ago.

"Believe me." What I tell you three times is true. True beyond any denial, true beyond any pain or guilt or fear or anything that might say no to it.

That time in Marrakech with Luka, we went down at nightfall to the Square of the Souls to watch a man push a thin metal skewer through his tongue from side to side while he danced and clicked his fingers and yelled praise to God. Each of those *believe me*s is like a thin, keen, leather-stropped skewer, driven through my lips, my tongue, the palm of each lying hand.


In the night the wind backs into the east, driving up great waves that shake Temple Twenty-four to its bedrock. A fine carrying wind for bicycle pilgrims, swirling us along the old coast path up through Temple Twenty-five to Twenty-six, flapping our henro robes like akira war banners. The sea below us is whipped up into long, foam-flecked combers; the pathside pines toss and blow. It is like riding through a Hiroshige print.

A kilometer out from Twenty-five we sight the clicking arthropod shape of Mr. Spider whirring along the henro path, corporate sponsorship logos bold and bright in the morning light, stole flying, bell chiming. He greets us warmly. He has been on the road since dawn—observing our bikes and outlandish garb, he comments that foot henro must have a good start under them before the day is too old. I cannot tell him that there is now a compact of secrecy between Mas and I as deep and dark as the compact of self-destruction he and I made on the cliff-top because I trusted his truth that the answer to misuse was not disuse—destruction—but right use. Name slips are exchanged—Mas's smartplastic gewgaw evokes a smile, but here we are first and last pilgrims meeting in a summer storm. He waves his staff as we pedal off up the path. *Dogyo Ninin.*

Rain had eroded the way into narrow, treacherous channels. My sudden braking sends the bike slewing across the henro path. Wet gravel crunches beneath my tires. Perplexed, Mas stops, pushes up his shades with gloved hand.

"Wait for me at Twenty-six," I shout to him over the wind roar. "Something I have to do. It's all right. Don't worry. Go on. Go. Scoot."

Alone with the wind and the rising ocean, I order one of my paper demons from the black box. The deep-throated mantra of the bell is heard before its bearer is seen. Presently, Mr. Spider tops the rise.

"Settai, Mr. Spider." I hold the folded slip of paper out to him.

"May this pilgrim ask what it is?" says Mr. Spider, settling with a hiss of hydrolastic struts into repose.

"A powerful talisman, bestowing health, vitality, and blessing upon all who meditate on it."

He laughs, swaying in his support cradle.

"It will need to be an exceedingly powerful talisman indeed." But he accepts it.

"When you no longer need it, pass it on to another," I tell him, though by that time the time-lock paper will have disintegrated. "Until then, you must not let another person see it."

"You can imagine a day when I will have no need for health, vitality, and blessing?"

Right toe into toe-clip, ready to push off. Wind eddies under the rim of my henro hat, lifting it. I could not have offered him the naked hope of regeneration, for he would not have dared accept something that, should it be false, would destroy him. Yet each time he contemplates Tiferet, it will slip past hopes and fears into the place where scarred, severed nerve fibers will grow again, where dead synapses will flicker and fire, bones strengthen, muscles firm and flex, legs walk.

"I can imagine that day," I say. At the point of the next headland I look back to admire the tiny, resolute figure—infinitesimal in this huge landscape—of Mr. Spider pressing on through the summer storm. I look, and I look, and I wait, and I watch, but there is no sign of him. No sign of him at all.

*We Two, Pilgrims Together.*


Because he told her to meet him in a Hi-Victorian majolica-tile waxed-wood and patinated-brass bar he despised; because when she arrived she found him alone in a booth drinking brandy that he detested, she knew what had happened. She let it work itself out under its own gravity; dark, cold subterranean waters following cracks and seams and fault lines.

"When I was eight my grandmother died," he began, twirling the stem of his brandy glass between thumb and forefinger. "She left me a pair of little ornaments that used to stand on her dressing table; a peasant boy whistling and a girl with a rabbit. They're on my bookshelf. You laughed at them. Cheap ornaments, the sort of thing you get on a day at the seaside; terminally tacky. But they outlived my grandmother, those two china ornaments. And they could outlive me. The life of Ethan Ring, passed into nothing, gone, forgotten, but still that barefoot girl would be cuddling her rabbit, that boy whistling down the wind with his hands in his pockets. It was like ice in my heart, that realization, like a huge, dark wall at the edge of life, so tall you couldn't get over it, so wide you couldn't get around it, overshadowing every waking thought and deed, and every day, every minute of every day, every tick of your watch, growing closer, taller, wider. For three months, I couldn't go anywhere, see anyone, do anything without seeing the shadow of mortality in them."

"We've immortality now," Luka said, thinking she gave comfort.

"We've ghosts and memories, for those that can pay."

Men in suits with digiphones and Olivetti/ICL Mark 88 bioprocessors folded into their inside pockets came crowding into the Hi-Victorian bar, cawing and crowing with that deliberate loudness particular to men in suits. With digiphones. And Olivetti/ICL Mark 88s.

"Marcus died this morning. Eighteen minutes past eleven."

"Fuck ... Ethan."

"At eleven-twelve he came out of the coma. At eleven-thirteen, he started convulsing. At eleven-eighteen, everything flat-lined. Twenty-three minutes later he was pronounced clinically dead and they took his liver and kidneys and pancreas. They left his heart and corneas. There was nothing left of them, they said. I was with him when he came out of it. For a moment he was himself, he was Marcus, waking up from a nightmare. Then it was as if he remembered something, saw something, a nightmare that blew out every neuron in his skull."

"Christ, Ethan ... the fracters."

Tracing the damp rings left by the glasses on the much-graffitied tabletop, Ethan Ring nodded.

"I caught a glimpse of it when I found him. It was like someone had hit me across the back of my neck with a piece of four by two. I couldn't walk, couldn't see properly for days after. God knows how long he'd been staring at it. Luka, I took the disk. I couldn't let them find it."

"Get rid of it, Ethan. Drop it in the river, dump it in a trash compactor, burn it, get rid of it. What I tell you three times is true. It's death." She took his face between her hands, then struck him hard across the cheek. Men in suits turned, made animal jeering noises.

"I'm sorry."

"Don't apologize." She struck him again. "Do it. Or you'll never see me again."

She had never looked so beautiful to Ethan as on the end of that blow.

For two days the disk sat in a Prisunic bag on his folding kitchenette-space table. On the evening of the second day, at about Soap Opera Time, she called him up.

"Have you done it yet?"

"Not yet; Luka, I'm still thinking ..."

She hung up.

For two days more the disk sat on top of the Prisunic bag on his folding kitchenette-space table. It kept creeping into his peripheral vision. At the start of the ads in the middle of Coronation Street, she called him again.

"Well, have you done it?"

"I'm going to, tomorrow, I promise ..."

She hung up.

For a further two days it sat in his backpack with a pair of hiking boots with the socks still stuffed into them while he vacillated between ax petrol deep water office block foundations. During one of those Great Scenes in the Rover's Return, she rang.

"Well?"

"Luka, it's not that simple ..."

"It's as simple as yes or no, Ethan."

"Luka ..."

Prrrrrrrrrrr.

"Luka!"

He took the backpack to a bus to a train to a biopower taxi to the door of the Nineteenth House and his co-mothers.

"It's Luka," said the sandwich Empress, recently out-franchised.

"He's got her pregnant," said the ex-dealer in Futures, anticipating new lives to welcome into the embrace of the kinship.

"He's in trouble with the cops," said the jewelry maker.

"It's drugs," said the telecommuting designer of European farming bulletins.

"No one gets busted for drugs anymore," said Nikki Ring.

"Well?" they all said.

"I'm all right," Ethan Ring said, which every mother knows for a lie when she hears it. "I need a little time to think things over."

The time ran out at four twenty-three A.M. at the dark end of the beach, where the lights of the condos and the yellow glow of the newly rebuilt marina did not reach. Trekking down with his backpack, Ethan encountered a man out running in astonishing rubber gear.

"Morning," said Ethan Ring. The man in astonishing rubber fled. Down where the tar-scabbed foam styrene and fragments of drift net washed up, he set down Marcus's disk, anointed it with paint thinners, and tore a match from a book bearing the crest of a doubtful Greek restaurant. A meteor crossed the sky.

"Fuck it."

He sent the matchbook, with its memories of souvlaki and salmonella, spinning after the fading meteor. Backpack heavy across one shoulder, he walked through the soft sand toward the lights of the town to tell Luka Casipriadin what he had done.

One week later, Luka Casipriadin applied for a transfer to the École des Beaux Arts et Desinées in Paris and moved out of the flat upstairs from Ethan Ring to address unspecified.


After ten years the smell of paint thinner has left the demon box. The certainties and dogmas of those years have likewise faded: from the Heisenbergian perspective of early thirtyhood I understand that Ethan Ring walking along that beach beneath the fall of early spring meteors must have had some compelling reason for not destroying the Sefirah disk. But I cannot remember what it was.

I find Mas's Dirt Wolf propped against a wall beside a public telecom bubble at Twenty-six. I tap the plastic to let him know I have arrived. Instantly, he cuts short his call and hangs up. English. I heard him speaking English. I note a number penciled on the User Information Chart: doodled Kabukimen identify it. A Yawatahama code.

"Who was that?" I ask. False innocence.

"Just a friend I haven't seen for some years," he answers. False ingenuousness. Liars both, we go up to the temple to pray for grace from the hands of Kobo Daishi. Armed and armored security police checking identities at the Shinto simulator look long and hard at us as we bypass the crowds and go up the shallow steps to the Butsu Hall. On their jackets and helmets is the eagle and lightning bolts of Tosa Securities Incorporated.


They came down for him as the band at the Thursday night spot in the deconsecrated church played its final cover. Since losing Luka, Ethan Ring had thrown himself into the regular class bacchanalias with the desperate enthusiasm of a man watching the trap of his own limitations close around him.

"Why won't she come back to me?" he confided to Kirstie-Lee, the class tramp who was wrapping her pink lycra thighs around his waist and her tongue around his cochlea because he might, sometime, someplace, be of Political Value to her.

And they came in through both sets of doors and fire exits. *What?* Chairs tables bottles rolling over *unh?* the band pulling plugs and hurrying backstage *"Luka!"* but it was in fact a big pig policeman spread-eagling him against the wall with the posters for legendary bands from the glittering 1970s, kicking his legs apart, fishing in his pockets *"What the . . . ?* and coming out with *something* between his fingertips, *something* that looked like a Ziploc plastic bag with *something* in it that looked exactly like marbley-red pills in the shape of winged cherub heads.

"Now, wot 'ave we 'ere, den?"

"You put them there," Ethan said, utterly incredulous. "You bastards!"

"Language, sir," said the big pig policeman spraying aerosol hallucinogens in Ethan Ring's face and tables chairs bottles band classmates and Kirstie-Lee unfolded into huge angel wings of light.

The toilet. That was the first thing. It was a metal slit in the floor.

The graffiti. That was the second thing. It was in a language full of doubled vowels, vaguely Hanseatic-looking.

The food. That was the third thing. It was exquisite. There was even a bottle of a beer he had never been able to justify on student budgets.

"Oh, Christ, I'm in Belgium," he said and threw up into the metal slit in the floor. When the last abreaction to the hallucinogens had passed, they came and took him from the rubber-floored cell to a woman with red glasses and lots of rings on her fingers, which she constantly twisted and turned. From the way she tilted her head toward him as he sat down in the comfortable chair he understood she was blind.

"Ghent, actually," she said in the idiomatic but slightly ungainly English of those not born to it.

"Ghent," Ethan Ring said. "What's in Ghent?"

"The European Common Security Secretariat."

"Isn't this a little excessive for a drugs bust?"

The blind woman smiled and from the drawer in her desk took a mega-density computer disk. It smelled faintly, but distinctly, of paint thinner.

"Oh, shit." Then, conclusions colliding like subatomic particles. "You broke into my flat. My flat ..."

"It fell into our bailiwick when the police resurrected the hard disk data your friend was working on before the, ah, accident? The police technician is out of intensive care, but it's debatable whether he will ever regain full control of his motor functions."

Nightmare trip. Someone had sold him something in the men's toilets and any moment now he would wake on his own or someone else's floor with a weapons-grade migraine.

"I must admit I'm a little disappointed in you, Mr. Ring. I'd expected more of the designer of these ..."

"Fracters. Lady, just who are you?"

The blind woman smiled with the minimalism of those who fear how much may be displayed on a face.

"We are a Research and Development Division of the European Common Security Secretariat. Our field of activity is psychological techniques."

"The fracters."

"Exactly, Mr. Ring. We know from Mr. Cranitch's notebooks of the existence of over one hundred fracters, as you call them, on that disk; psychological weapons of a power and refinement that makes our current projects look as sophisticated as Halloween masks and calling rude names."

"You went through Marcus's room? You picked through his stuff?"

"Mr. Ring, you really will have to learn to be less scrupulous when you are working for us."

"I don't remember agreeing to any prospective employment."

"It's a simple either/or, Mr. Ring. The 'either' is: Go back to university. Complete your course. Get your qualification. Keep the computer. Keep the fracter programs. You have the passwords: keep them. We will give you a job in European Public Relations, pay you, protect you, keep you safe. In return for this, use the fracters for us when we need them. It will not be often. It may be never.

"The 'or' is: Take your chances with the White Americans, the Pacific Rimmers, Pan-Islam. Frankly, I can't see them taking time to have this discussion with you. Tell me, how long do you think you could bear to watch your girlfriend—what's she called, Luka Casipriadin—what is that, Armenian, Georgian?—how long could you watch her being raped by dogs? Two hours? Four hours? Eight, even? And once they had what they wanted I think you'd find they'd forget about any gentleman's agreements they might have made. A bullet in the left eye is current *mode d'emploi* of the PRCPS Security corporations."

"You're not frightening me," he said, which is only ever said by those who are very, very afraid.

The blind woman set a black cellphone on the desk beside the Sefirah disk.

"Call her. Luka Casipriadin. It should be breakfast time; she always was a late riser. I don't see how she stomachs that bran mush muck every day when they do excellent croissants in the École refectory. I suppose the

Californian raisins help. The code from Ghent for Paris is 00 33 1."

"Fuck you, you bitch. Fuck you to hell."

"You're welcome to try, Mr. Ring. Do you want to accept now or think about it?"

"Is there any point?"

"Should I take that to be an affirmative?"

"You should."

"I'm glad, Mr. Ring. You see, there is a small button on the arm of my chair that I really didn't want to have to press. I was a little ... economical with the truth. We couldn't really have let you take the 'or' option and gone to the Yankees, or the Islamics. The side of the desk facing you conceals a compressed-gas-powered guillotine—most sharp." She left her seat, came around the desk. Her fingers brushed Ethan Ring's thigh, spidered up two steps above his navel. "It would have cut you cleanly in two"—her fingers tapped black denim shirt still smelling of beer, smokes, and spray-crazy—"just about here."

Tappy tap.


If it were Ethan Ring making this pilgrimage, he would observe that life is a circular pilgrimage from nothingness to nothingness, the Temple Zero of nonexistence, up the steep ascents of circumstance and Murphy's Law to mountaintops of self-realization, down long easy descents when sore spirits can relax from pushing the intractable mechanism of living on through history, from dark sea caverns of acedia, filled with the ocean-sound of mortality to six-lane highways crammed with rushing, prehistoric behemoths.

Strange: the more I re-create of the life of Ethan

Ring, the less there is of him that I can recognize in me. Some grace of Kobo Daishi, that I can no longer draw absolutes from particulars as he once would have in self-justification. My homily would be that the Buddha-head rests as comfortably in the Shinamo gear-train of a twenty-four-speed MTB as in the face of Kokuzo carved into the flesh of a living tree and that the temples of true, real, burning *living* are so few and far between that we must hold hard to our sacred moments.

Long hard haul down the south coast of Muroto. Only four temples between the West Temple and Kochi City; there would be much room for the contemplation of the Buddha of the gear-train were it not that our way lies along the main provincial highway. A fifty-meter cloudbase discharges a steady, penitential drizzle; thundering truck/trailer combos spray us with a viscous film of oily grit. At a *bangai* incorporated into a syrup-station and travel lodge we are given settai of tea and tangerines by the proprietor: a brief blessing. Then: smog masks and wraparounds; helmet down and push.

When we find a bas-relief finger on a squat pillar pointing down a muddy footpath through birches and alders, it is like the manifestation of the saint himself. Joyfully we turn off the road and hurtle as fast as we can down the old path among the birch trees.

The henro path leads us into a rich, timeless agricultural landscape. We cycle through grass-roofed villages, along narrow causeways between flooded paddies where mud-smeared wading robots tend crops of tall, slender shoots—tatami reeds, Mas informs me. Absurdly, I feel like the hero in a spaghetti Western. Though my plastic rainsheet bestows some characteristics of the Man With No Name, this awareness comes not from any change in myself, but in my surroundings, so pervasive yet subtle it is several kilometers farther before I can pinpoint it. On every house. On every shop. On every vehicle and robot and biogas plant and windpump and gatepost and signpost: the mark of the eagle and the lightning: *Protected by Tosa Securities Incorporated.*

"Like a set from a Kurosawa movie," agrees Mas, drawing alongside. Troubled in spirit, we press on and the rain steepens into a general downpour.

In an attempt to expose us to a wider world than typography and corporate logos, the mandarins of Graphic Communications decreed that we attend weekly lectures on whatever particular hobbyhorse the tutorial staff liked to ride. The only one I remember was Jake Byrne, our year tutor, proposing his outrageous/rightwing/racist/xenophobic theory of sociological inertia. *Reader's Digest* condensed version: national characteristics as bred in bone as hair/eyes/coloring: re *Japan:zaibatsus* collapse, arcologies burn, Euro/Islamic graverobbers dismember, honorable salaryperson throws *off* business suit *out* come swords/armor/helmet waiting in the attic, hello boys it's the Last Remake of *Kagemusha: the Shadow Warrior.* If Masahiko can no longer see the Japan of his childhood in the Japan of his thirty-somethings, perhaps we should not be surprised to find this prosperous farming land the fiefdom of some neo-feudal private security company.

I feel very far from the Approved Tourist Route.

The inscription tells us that the shrine has stood for three hundred and twenty-eight years, and implies that it will be here long after the incongruous modern green of a private golf course straddling the henro path has returned to nature again. Its guardian is newer, and more transient, than even the golf course. Mas dismounts, crouches down, obscenely fascinated. His raincape sheds sheets of water. Small tearing animals have ripped away lips, cheeks, eyes; the ears have been reduced to two knobs of gnawed gristle. Where it has been tattooed, the skin has remained intact by virtue of some preservative feature of the inks. The plastic helmet is impervious to both elements and animals, the plastic ident tag likewise, concealed among early summer's burst of rainwet bluebells, aconites, and wild garlic. On the edge of the rough, the head of the young akira keeps watch on the plaid trousers and Mr. Dormie club-bags and biopower golf karts. Are the junior account managers and sales executives applauding beneath their corporate golf umbrellas—*golfu* is too important a thing to be surrendered to a mere monsoon—when Mr. Chairman hits one straight down the middle aware of the barbarism not a hundred meters from the thirteenth tee? What are the Acceptable Levels for an uninterrupted round of Royal and Ancient?

Mas has found an accountholder's plastic smartcard among the wet spring flowers. Embossed on its plastic face is the ubiquitous thunder-eagle of Tosa Securities Inc.

"Christ's sake, Mas, leave it." Foolish pilgrim, who does not recognize an omen.

It is only a few hundred meters across rough, fairway, and Number Thirteen green—we can see the marker stone at the edge of the woodlands, the henro path itself wending into the trees—but among the golf karts puttering and stuttering over the grass is a blue and white buggy adorned with ToSec's thunder-eagle. The angularities of light-power armor beneath Adidas trackwear are visible from our position on the edge of the rough. I cannot see enforcers who tear off a trespassing akira's head taking kindly to two henro leaving tire tracks across the apron of the par three Number Thirteen.

We are effectively stymied. We cannot go forward, we will not go back, not twenty kilometers through Clint Eastwood country to the Tourist Route again. Therefore, we go around. Golf courses only seem to go on forever. A hundred or so meters back, past the dark shrine, we find a path—little more than trampled vegetation—headed in what seems like generally the right direction. After twisting and turning through riotous vegetation running wild in expectation of summer the trail plunges headlong into a vast sugarcane plantation. The rain patters on the alien cane. We have no idea where we are going; we trust that a straight path must have a destination. After ten minutes—not so much a plantation, this, as a monoculture—we hit a wide access route and come out of the claustrophobic cane on top of the cane farmer himself engaged in some cannicultural activity involving standing in the back of a Nissan pickup.

Guilty both legally and spiritually of trespass we accelerate past him before he can protest. At the sound of a shouting voice I glance over my shoulder. The farmer is waving something in his hand—I cannot be certain at this distance but it has the hard glitter of electronics. What is he shouting? Dogs? What about them?

Hydrogas shocks notwithstanding, the bike rattles as it takes the ruts, and I glance back again, just for an instant. The farmer is in his pickup now, driving after us. I shout to Mas but he has already seen and, one foot thrust out as a brake, skid-turns ninety degrees into a narrow file where no pickup can follow.

Dogs?

*Somethings.* Fragments of movement. Discordant patterns of light and shade within the regularity of the head-high sugarcane. Glimpses. Glances. Flickers. More than five, I reckon, less than twenty. And not human. Too low, too fast, too relentless to be human. Mas too senses them; a glance is the signal for us to flick into high gear. The hunters in the cane match us without a flicker of hesitation. I hear Mas swear. I glance back. Dogs. A hunting pack of ten, closing on us. Cancerous bulbs of bioprocessor implants blister their skulls; each wears the unmistakable ToSec logo spray-painted on its chest.

That hint of electronics I had seen in the farmer's hand was a command unit.

That time, in Marrakech, Luka took me to a dog pit in the old city. Under the white heat of the kilowatt floods we watched the augmented dogs tear and rip and spray red arterial blood over the front rows. We watched them die on the bloody sand and still they tore at each other, enslaved even beyond death to the commands pouring from their sweating, screaming masters' control gloves.

Except this man was not threatening us. He was warning us.

Mas's sudden brake and swerve almost sends me into him. A hundred or so meters ahead, a second pack of augmented dogs is bounding toward us with elegant, deadly fluidity.

I have seconds. Only seconds ...

"Close your eyes!" I shout to Mas and they are on us. The lead dog leaps. I meet it with my naked left hand. It spins into the cane, neck broken, writhing, yelping hideously.

If the right hand is truth, what is the left?

Answer: destruction. Keter: the Void, Annihilation,

the shock fracter. Animal, human, artificial intelligence: whatsoever has eyes to see, it will destroy.

Wherever I turn my left hand, dogs jerk and spasm and fall. They are savage, they are deadly, but those are not enough, not against an enemy that attacks on sight. Five. Ten. Fifteen. Twenty. In as many seconds. The cane field is littered with twisted meat, kicking in the red mud. Slipping between close-packed cane, I go from dog to dog, clamping my left hand over each face until the spasms stop. Mercy mercy. On its side in a drainage ditch, a dog beats its stump tail weakly, watches, panting, with puppy-dog eyes free from the unclean light of simulated sentience. Its breath is warm on my skin. *Hush, hush there,* I whisper in English as I press my left hand over its eyes. It jerks. Once.

A sugarcane farmer, however large his holding, could not afford twenty cybercanines. A time-share and a control unit, yes, but the true owners, the true masters, are elsewhere and cannot be oblivious of what has happened to their property. Or of us. Why would a farmer who had warned us of his dogs not stop them with his command unit? Unless, in a higher place, control was taken away from him, by someone who knew exactly what he/she/it was looking for.

Crouching, hands over eyes (See-No-Evil), Mas flinches at the touch of my hand on his shoulder.

"It's over, Mas. Let's go." I want this thunder-eagle country and the evil it has forced me into far behind me. Curled around the thick, padded handlebars, my palms burn as if freshly branded. All masters of the dark arts agree: there is a terrible, seductive joy in the practice and use of their power. It felt good all those other times when I used my power, when I felt like God, that there was no authority on earth could deny me. The masters never mention that there is a price for that thrill, as there is a price for everything, and the price is pain. It can be emotional, it can be spiritual, it can be physical. But it never misses. The pain will always find you. It cannot be begged off, bargained with, wished away.

We first met in a large, high-ceilinged, windowless room, the pain and I, echoing and resonant, the kind of room where the door merges into the wall behind you and seems never to have been. Gray. All gray. The chair: gray. The Bosch industrial robot: gray. The only color: the dyes in their plastic tubes; the needles poised above them.

"Will it hurt?" the blind woman in the red glasses asked as she strapped my wrists to the arms of the gray chair, opened the fingers one two three four and thumb five, taped them down.

"It will hurt," I said and because she was that particular kind of coward that cannot bear another's pain, she slipped the disk into the robot and closed the door behind her.

The physical pain was the least part. The true pain was the sense of violation, that the dyes the flicking needles were stitching into the palms of my hands were spreading through my bloodstream, along my nerve fibers, branding me within as indelibly as I was marked without. In Kafka there is a long and terrible story about some engine of execution that wrote a man's crimes into his flesh with needles. Crimes past: but what about crimes yet to be committed? Can the punishment precede the crime? If there is a point at which the long death and rebirth of Ethan Ring is focused, it is the points of those five colored needles.

Burning. My hands are burning so hot I am afraid to look at them. I want to stop. I want to cry out. I want to plunge them into deep, cold water. Guilt. Burning. Heat. Heat is an energy, energy I can use to push me on, push me away, push me through to the place beyond guilt. Push through. Push through. Or the things you have sealed up inside another life will push through into you. Into him. Into me. Me. Him.

Suzy Magee Annett, age size and three-quarters, westbound with her mother to some kind of marital reconciliation by the ocean, had stared for most of the semi-orbital flight at the new plastic socket one and one half centimeters behind the lobe of Ethan Ring's right ear, ringed by a halo of red itching scar tissue to which the eye could not but be drawn because they had shaved half his skull to accommodate it.

"Mummy Mummy Mummy that man's got a hole in his head," said Suzy Magee Annett, unable to contain herself any longer, and was told not to be so nosy about other people and go to sleep and when he thought they were finally asleep he took out the tap and slipped it into the socket and so learned that the European Pacific Rim network had uncovered a Pan-Islamic mole and that he was being sent to find out what he knew and take it away from him. Except that Suzy Magee Annett was a bad little girl and watched through half-closed eyes the disgusting fascinating spectacle of a man with a worm in his head.

They had the man in one of the last Barbary Coast wooden houses to escape the Race Wars. He was naked and fastened to a deeply beautiful Shaker chair with brown adhesive tape, which seemed excessive to Ethan Ring. He was a deeply beautiful man.

"Leave me," said Ethan Ring, picking at the flaking

skin around his implant. He showed the man his right hand and said, "Tell me your secrets."

While the man taped to the Shaker chair spooled off names and addresses and informants and dead drops into a microtaper, Ethan Ring printed out the Hokhmah fracter and hid it in the palm of his gloved left hand.

"Forget it," he said, opening his left hand. And it was gone.

"That's it," he told the others, handing them the microcassette.

"Good," they said. "Now do the rest. Take it all away."

"Everything?" he said.

"Everything. We want them to be afraid of us. Very afraid of us."

So he went back to the naked man and took away all the numbers that might have identified him. License, passport, ID, Social Security, buckcard, credit accounts, e-mail, street name and number, locker number. Gone.

His friends. Gone.

His lovers. Gone.

His enemies. Gone.

His brothers, his sisters, his aunts and uncles and cousins and father and mother. Gone.

The next day Ethan Ring came and peeled the last ten years of his life off like the rind of an orange. College years. Dawn at Zabriskie Point. The time at the Faculty Club pool. The time on the floor in Belsize Park. The adrenaline ecstasy of making it to the top of Half Dome. Getting drunk in Paris in the rain. Dancing in the snow at Noo Year. Gone.

Teenage years, high school angst and acne, first fucks. Gone.

Vertiginous adolescence as the vast incoherencies of the adult world began to make sense. Gone.

Childhood, prechildhood, the neural rainforest of memories, impressions, sensations he had forgotten he had ever forgotten. Gone.

The third day Ethan Ring took away everything he knew. How to drive a car. How to speak Spanish. How to cook an omelet, how to ride a bicycle. The names of the twelve nearest stars. Gone. The words to old Elvis Costello songs. Gone. The interstate route map and the Northwest Pacific domestic timetable. Gone. Walt Whitman. Emily Dickinson. The Trout Quintet. Meat Loaf. Gone. History. Geography. Physics. Chemistry. Biology. Art. Music. Gone. Reading. 'Riting. 'Rithmatic. Gone.

Only one thing remained.

"Tell me your name."

"Titus Witters. My name is James Titus Witters," said the naked man taped into the wooden Shaker chair. "Please, man, not that, leave me that ..."

Gone.

"He's yours now," said Ethan Ring. He got into his hire car, tried to drive back to his hotel, and got caught in the twelve-block gridlock caused by Mrs. Marta Radetczy age sixty-eight's inadvertent stepping into the path of a V.W./G.M. biopower Bagels'R'Us truck. Otherwise he would have driven past the Pendereski Gallery without noticing that it was celebrating *that very night* the gala opening of a new work, entitled *Fantasia*, by hot hot new talent Luka Casipriadin.

He thought the suit made him look like a riverboat gambler but the man in the hire shop was adamant that it was very suave, very chic, very sir, sir. From the far side of the crowded room she recognized him—his undisguisable red hair, he supposed, even more conspicuous half shaved away—and came cutting cleanly through the shoals of society/charity/arty/party/drinky/dopey and doc.

"You look like a riverboat gambler." She ran the palm of her hand along the line of his jaw.

"You look like a dream found in a gutter one hour before dawn, down with the needles and guns and dead." He ran his fingers through the short stubble on either side of her crest of black hair.

"I love it when you talk mucky," she said, drawing him away through the throng of cocktail glasses, lip gloss, and Cartier pill-cases. Her fingers caressed his socket. "Your bosses must think a lot of you to fit you up with one of these. Come on. Got something to show you. Preview of coming attractions. For your eyes only." Outside on the fire escape a light drizzle was falling. She swung over the rail and dropped into the neon-shadowed alley, landing surefooted, cat-coiled. A two-finger whistle: "Yo! Oddjob! To me!"

Stirrings in the shadows, clicking, whirrings, a gleam of light from a polished surface. A Dornier Hi-performance Industrial Robot stepped into the alley, bobbing on cantilever legs, gleaming yellow carapace spotted with rain. Luka rested a black gloved hand on its curved plastic skull.

"Here. Catch." She skimmed a black something up at him. A snatch of immaculate kid-gloved hands: an Olivetti/IBM Mark Twenty VR-tap.

"The difference between this new bioprocessor stuff and the old clunky noninvasive gear has to be experienced to be believed," she said. "Obviously, you were sent by God; Ethan Ring in San Francisco with a shiny new hole in his head. You get the deluxe wide-screen edition. One word of warning: be not fooled by the name. Fucking Walt Disney this isn't."

Fucking Walt Disney this wasn't.

"We've all got them," Luka explained as they slipped through the rain-wet streets, splashing through puddles of neon Timor and Vietnamese, the riverboat gambler and the fetish queen with their robot skipping behind. "But we're afraid of them, we're afraid that if people find out they'll think we're dark and evil and perverted or silly and stupid and fatuous, while in their own heads, those other people are exactly the same. Exactly the same." Around them fin de siècle brownstones and leery chromium-age office blocks erupted into organic volcanoes of lilac-scented blossoms or stretched into window-studded trees whose trunks upheld the cotton-candy sky; manhole covers became smirking demon faces; every mailbox was a welcoming vagina with lolling forked tongue and grazing pedicabs, bizarre bucolic hybrids half man/half bicycle, bounded like startled gazelles from predatory taxis circling like checkerboard sharks.

"The processing equipment's aboard Oddjob; we're hooked in real-time through a mega-plex infrared link. Micro-cameras on the headband. Come a long way from Umberto Boccioni." The Bay Bridge uprooted booted feet and went buckarooing over Oakland while a fifteen-year-old girl confessed a long and labyrinthine dream into Ethan Ring's middle ear. Luka pulled him toward the gateway of a covered market that shapeshifted into ideogram-stained teeth, a swallowing neon-lit maw. Within, the biogas-lit stalls with their pendulous racks of edibles and smokables became the pulsing organs of a post-cybernetic bodyscape; the bustling crowd, shouting in a dozen different Southeast Asian dialects, were swarms of platelets, macrophages, and antibodies.

Above the inner voice of a man describing a fantastic mescalin voyage beneath the linked geodesics of his own skin, Ethan shouted, "You're a sick woman, Luka Casipriadin."

"These aren't my head dreams," she shouted back. "This is some poor bastard of an HIV IV victim's dream of one final DPMA trip into himself to battle the disease that has, by now, probably killed him. They're all live. All real. 0898 FANTASY—at the tone leave your darkest dream, your brightest hope, confess it to Luka absolute confidentiality assured."

"Except you blow it up over three city blocks and people pay to have it shoved through a little hole in their heads."

"They all knew what I wanted to do with their fantasies. Logged five thousand calls in the three months I kept the line open. Tapped some deep, dark confessional urge in the population of the Greater Bay Area. You think I'm sick, you should hear some of the ones I didn't use. I'd like to think that some of my sources will come and look at it and feel that their openness about their fantasies will help other poor repressed bastards."

"Even for you that is a singularly weak self-justification."

"Isn't it just?"

The puckered, neon-spangled rectum of the market shat them and their yellow Dornier out at the foot of twenty stories of First Pacific Rim Bank morphing into a naked twenty-year-old man with fabulous black hair and muscles. As a fifty-something woman's voice whispered sweet sexual imaginings to the accompaniment of a reconstructed Julie Andrews singing a pornographic version of "Favorite Things" ("Naked black sailors all tied up with string"), powerlines snapped and came twining through the air to coil and knot around the straining leviathan.

"Fucking hell," said Ethan Ring, thinking of the man in the Shaker chair in the last wooden house in San Francisco.

Onward.

Through faerylands and Disneylands and *petit* Arcadias two blocks by three, heavens and hells, through blizzards of dollar bills while palm trees bent their mop heads close together and sang old Prince numbers in close harmony and cathedrals took off like gothic rockets beneath skies filled with plump Georges Méliès desmoiselles dressed as shooting stars and comets until, beneath a floodlit Coit Tower ecstatically transubstantiating into a Hieronymous Bosch cromlech/mushroom/phallus complete with dancing nymphs, flying sharks and goose-stepping storks, she kissed him. Hard. In the mouth. With much tongue.

"I could tie you up with string," she said and pulled the tap out of his skull and vanished all dreams and yearnings and fantasies in a candy-colored pop! "Ethan, I'm sorry. Those years, what I did to you. I'm a coward. I'm like Buddha, I like to think I'm living in a perfect painless world of art and artifice, then comes the first sign of hurt and I press disengage. Fuck, even for me, that's a singularly weak self-justification. Okay, Ethan Ring, here I am, if you'll have me." She slapped the Dornier's yellow shell. "Get the hell home, Oddjob."

They ate things cooked in aluminum foil in a Timorese sampan restaurant. They took a mopedcab down through the old Italian and slightly less old Vietnamese and newer Indonesian and new North Australian and newest Southern-States-white-trash-shanty districts to the bridge where they told the driver to wait for them, which meant that they were not going to go halfway and throw themselves off. They drank bourbon in a bar and got drunk but not too. They went back to Ethan Ring's towertop suite with its view over the Euclidian geometry of city lights interrupted by the Mandelbrotian mathematics of the Bay.

"Wouldn't you love to stand naked in front of that window?" Luka said, sitting on his bed and heaving and grunting at her boots. Ethan slipped off his riverboat gambler's jacket and brocade waistcoat and was unfastening his pearl shirt buttons when she noticed.

"That would be a lot easier if you took your gloves off."

A pause, while something like a spiked fist reached into his chest and tore out his heart.

"Ethan, what have you done with your hands, Ethan?"

He told her. His head reverberated to a vertiginous white roar as he told her about what he had done to his hands, to himself, to the man in the Shaker chair. He stood at the window and watched the transparent dirigibles filled with cold-gas holograms for diet Coke and Volkswagen-G.M. and Chanel 15 drift across the beautiful city until he heard the door click shut and lock behind him.


Raw fire; burning down my throat. I cough, retch, *fire* goes down into my lungs. I spew up a spray of phlegm and bile and burning.

"It's all right, Eth. Take it easy." Another splash of liquid heat across my lips, down my throat. Distant monosyllables; Japanese. "Old Suntory, Eth. For the shock."

*Mas.* My voice is a ghastly rattlesnake rasp. I push the glass away.

"You're all right now. The Tanazakis say we can stay here until you are able to go on." Feeling behind my right ear my fingers encounter only the plastic disk of an empty socket. *Touch* solidifies the unfocused color field surrounding me into objects: a rectangle of light is a window filled with concrete-colored sky, a lozenge of fitful cerise and lilac a neon sign, a circle in the bottom right corner of the streaming window: a sticker. PROTECTED BY TOSA SECURITIES INCORPORATED. I try to struggle free from the bed; Mas's hand is on my chest.

"Easy, Eth. You've had a bad shock."

"Mas ..."

"You came off the bike. You hit a rut. You were riding like ... like something possessed, a demon. It's a miracle you weren't impaled on the cane."

The dogs. The cane field. I remember. A young woman—eighteen, twentyish—enters with tea.

"The farmer got you into the back of the pickup and brought you here. You were shaking all over. Like a fit. Like epilepsy."

That's the bargain it makes. You use it, it uses you, and more, each time. I take the cup of tea between my gloved hands, savor the good, clean scald of it.

"I've called her, Eth. She's hiring a car, she'll be here by morning. She'll be able to help you."

*She?* I want to ask, *she?* but a middle-aged woman has appeared at the side of the bed and is pressing self-adhesive tranquilizer dots to my acupuncture points. *She ...?*


Bible Stories for Buddhists: The Good Samaritan found the traveler by the side of the road and brought him to an inn. In the three hundred and twelve years since

Ruichi Tanazaki I, inspired by a vision of the face of the Daishi in the tea leaves at the bottom of a bowl, opened his teahouse for the succor of weary henro, successive generations have added and enlarged and expanded until now the Tanazaki-ya stands as a marvelous miscegeny moteldinergaragegiftshopgasstationpharmacybathhouse-barbershopkaraokeparlorcathousepickupjoint; a true and honest tribute to the spirit of vernacular building that finds its highest expression in roadside architecture. The Smithsonian should have it heli-lifted whole and pre-served, with its motley, polyglot crew of Tanazakis, gen-erations ten through twelve, for the delight and elucidation of future, poorer descendants. Wandering in post-tranq blur through the warren of extensions, an-nexes, and additions trying to find Mas, I feel like an unnoticed animal stowing away on some surreal ark sail-ing up through history. I keep arriving in the same bar snug where a small peer group of salarypersons with their jackets off are toasting each other and singing along to a sat-tel pop channel. Every time, they are that little bit drunker, that little bit more nicely out of tune.

The diner is unlit save for the neons along the self-serve bar and the unregarded television glow from the booth where Mas is talking with the girl who brought me tea. They are the sole occupants. Comic book on poles and crushed plastic beer cans litter the melamine tabletop: I feel vaguely blasphemous at having inter-rupted a private moment. Mas introduces the girl, Mariko. The perfect hostess, she bows and brings beer from the cool cabinet; very cold, very good.

"Mas. How long has Luka been here?"

He offers me one from his pack of Tiger Tails.

"She was held up in Tokyo. She came down here

the day before yesterday. We were to meet her in Yawatahama."

I breathe in the smoke from the *cañabarillo*, let it fry my head, just a little, let it knock me loose from the things that have been closing around me so inexorably. If you are going to sin, henro, then sin big, so that grace may all the more abound.

"It was her you were talking to, those long-distance calls. No wonder you switched the picture off."

On the television, sumo wrestlers bump and grind silently in the sacred clay ring.

"It was planned long before Temple One. Back to that time you met in Capetown, when you told her you were thinking seriously of taking up my suggestion of the pilgrimage."

"My God. A cozy little conspiracy. Where did you dream all this up, in bed together in some capsule hotel with a bottle of sake and pornographic comics?"

Though I know the depth of anger of which Mas is capable, the sudden nova-flare of it is still frightening.

"Do not ever, ever, talk about her that way. Ever, you bastard. Maier-Mikoyan commissioned a virtuality from her, up in Sapporo for the Ice Fest. We met there. She thought that the pilgrimage might be a way for you to break free. Save yourself, save your soul."

"Well hallelujah for little Miss Salvation Army. So you knew about me all along. Was all that stuff, back at Muroto, made up for me too?"

For a moment I am certain, certain, that if there were anything sharper than a disposable chopstick to hand, Mas would have buried it in my throat.

"I don't know what she sees in you. You are selfish, ungrateful, vicious, cowardly. You're a child, Eth. She didn't give away any of your fucking state secrets. You did that. You can't even be trusted not to betray your country. She just said you were in trouble. Powerful trouble, and the pilgrimage might give you the space and strength to break free; that was all. And for some reason, I agreed to help her.

"She loves you. She has never loved anyone else and will never love anyone else and you hurt her. You have hurt her, you hurt her now, you will go on hurting her."

"Oh, Christ, Mas."

Voices, in the lobby. Mr. Tanazaki, and two others. Loud voices. Strong voices. Dangerous voices. I half rise, half turn in my seat, and they burst in through the door. Meat. Heavies. Akiras, two of. Camouflage parkas undecided between sickly neon and midnight black. Hair scraped back and thonged into oily pigtails. Wraparound visors streaked with alphanumerals; raster lines closing around my image.

I am on my feet, hands curled into loose fists in an instant of primal reaction. Laser sights paint red caste marks on my forehead and heart. Airborne dust traces them back to the Fiuzzi automatic pistols.

"You. You." One red thread dances away to rest on the bridge of Mas's nose. "With us."

Shouting protest, Mr. Tanazaki tries to snatch a weapon. The red beam weaves over booths, ceiling, floor, then with the frightening casualness of chemically enhanced strength, the akira slams him against the cooler cabinet, smashes him with the butt of his weapon, smashes him, smashes him, smashes him. There is screaming in the lobby.

And I open my left hand.

Keter sends the akira—spasming, jerking, shivering—into the wall. In a flicker of violence, I am on top of him. All I know, all I understand, all I feel, is the anger, the years of anger, burning along my arm, drawing into a knot of white heat at the center of my left hand. I imagine my left hand pressed over his eyes and unholy joy blazes through me.

"Ethan! Leave him!" Mas. The second akira sends the searching finger of his targeting laser after me; I roll away, come into a crouch, left hand ready.

"No, Eth. Not this way."

No. This is not the way. It was the way of Ethan Ring. It is not your way. My way. My hand opens like a lotus blooming. My right hand.

"Put the gun down." The voice of absolute authority does not need to shout. Click of ceramics and steel on the floorboards. The laser sight draws a strict red terminator across the polished wood. "Squat down. On your heels. Hands on head. Stay that way until I tell you otherwise."

He obeys. He cannot but. His camouflage parka turns cold neon blue.

"Who sent you?"

"Tosa Securities Aki Section Manager, on the instructions of the Chief Security Executive. Our Chapter are subcontractees."

The classic pattern, divide and recruit your enemies. If even akiras serve and find it no dishonor, this land is more firmly in Tosa Securities' fist than I had imagined. We cannot afford to remain even one hour more. Mrs. Tanazaki, Mariko, and eldest son are kneeling beside Mr. Tanazaki. There is a lot of blood and he does not move. Mrs. Tanazaki is rocking back and forth, back and forth, back and forth. Younger son is making a call on the lobby desk phone.

"No!" I shout. "Leave it!" His fingers hesitate over the touch buttons, then decide. "Look at me," I order, right hand upheld. In the dark lobby, his pupils dilate. "Leave it." The voicepiece clicks into its cradle.

"It was only an ambulance," he says. Mariko looks at me with such hatred it is like a rod of frozen iron thrust up my spine. My Healing and Tranquillity fracters could help Mr. Tanazaki until we are gone and it is safe to call an ambulance but Mariko would not accept my gift and anyway I cannot spare the few minutes it would take to print them out.

The pilgrimage is over. Destroyed. It was destroyed the first time I typed the words *what I tell you three times is true* in that dark room in the Morikawa farmhouse.

"Mas, we must go."

"No, Ethan." The refusal strikes like a bullet. "It's always been shit and walk away, hasn't it? Cycle into people's lives, do your tricks, and cycle out again. These are the people who get left behind. Everything they have is here. They can't leave when it all starts to slide. You come into their world, in one evening destroy it, and the next morning when the ToSec investigators come to find out what happened to their akiras, you are on your knees in some temple sanctuary praying for the Daishi to shrive your sins and enlighten your spirit. You don't understand, you Europeans cannot understand; there is no higher principle, no unalienable human right to which they can appeal. No noble Western notion of fairness and justice and innocence until proved guilty. Tosa Securities is the law here."

A bullet. A slow bullet chewing through bone and flesh and gristle into the heart of me with the cold, precipitous knowledge that those unshakable foundations of absolute law and the incorruptibility of its agents upon which my society rests complacently do not exist here. For most of human history; and now again, in this time of the fading of Western Industrial Democracy, law has been—is now—the province of power.

Once Mother Emma—the sandwich Empress— showed me how to catch shrews in a glass bottle. Enticed by catfood, they were lured into the neck (so far, so good) and down into the belly (so far, so better). Only after gorging themselves on liver-and-kidney Whiskas did they realize that they could not climb the smooth, sloping glass shoulders to the neck. Trapped. I had thought myself free, but it had been the illusion of smooth, transparent walls. History: my own, that of the land through which I have been pursuing my own enlightenment, drew me onward, downward, to the thrill of playing with demons from which there is no return. Trapped.

My fists hammer melamine tabletop.

"There has to be an end to it, don't you see, Mas? There has to be a way to live that doesn't have violence as the solution to every question. I know what you're asking, Mas. This is life. This isn't a Kurosawa movie, this isn't *Anime*. I said it at Turtle Beach, I say it again here, I am not fucking Kabukiman. We're not paint or pixels or whatever the hell you use, we're flesh, we're blood. We die."

Even as I speak I see the Tanazakis and behind them in the lobby, unseen, unpaying, guests. Mr. Morikawa killed by his naive belief in the inviolability of authority. The dispossessed of Tokushima, of all Japan, victims of misplaced faith in the chaotic gods of economics, and the akiras, the kids who hadn't sold themselves to their enemies because they still believed in a mythic, perfect past. A nameless wind-cured head on a stick by a Kochi wayside shrine. Mas's lover in her kneepads, elbow guards, and tight, cute volleyball shorts, killed by a dream of California. Others. Hundreds upon hundreds of others. Nameless, faceless, historyless, the payers of tolls and tithes and taxes, the buyers of permits and licenses and visas, the ones who bleed for a law that does not protect them.

I see a saint handing me a shot at redemption, a chance to pit my power not against the abstract, utilitarian pseudo-evils of planetary economics and *welt*-political expediency, but against actual, tangible, pragmatic, mundane tyranny. Evil. Simple. Straight. Undisguised and unambiguous. And with the chance to leave the world a different—better—place after from before. It always was heroes and angels, Luka. And I look away. I look away and so see him, reflected in the back bar mirror. Death dwells in mirrors; with every look, it grows a little, every day. Death, change, time. He is a tall man in his early thirties with wild red hair tied back. From the far side of the silvered glass where I banished him so he could never hurt me again, Ethan Ring beckons. He is me. I must embrace him. Accept him. What other way could it be? *Dogyo Ninin.* We Two, Pilgrims Together.


Scissors cut, snip, snip. The red hair falls in long red coils to the flagstones of the courtyard garden. I lift a lock, the clean, bright scissors cut, it falls. Preparations for battle matter. Medieval knights-errant spent the night before their elevation at the altar in prayer.

I had Mr. Tanazaki installed in his bedroom with the angels of Tranquillity and Healing set at his head and feet to watch over him. Son Nobuo is watching over the comatose akira in a guestroom in an unused wing; in the next room I have put the second akira and set the angel Binah, the fracter that annihilates chronoconsciousness, on the back of the door to hold him frozen in time.

Every demon was at some time an angel. The half-life built into the unstable paper will keep the world safe from demons, or angels.

Built-in decay. Indeed.

Snip. Another piece of me falls. The garden may be no more than a handful of square meters of courtyard between two residential wings but all the world is here. A pool for ocean, rocks rising from fine, raked gravel mountains in the desert; a forest of bamboo, a stone lantern filled with bioluminescents for moon and the shrine to the generations of dead Tanazakis the spiritual focus. Early jasmine, late magnolia perfumes the air; the rain has ended, the night is supernaturally warm and still. *What am I going to tell Luka if you get killed?* Masahiko had asked.

See you in another life, Luka.

I run my fingers over the ragged stubble of my scalp. My preparations are almost complete. All I need now is one final piece of memory, the keystone, lowered into position and the bridge between what I was and what I am will be complete.

The theory was that at any instant in political history there are two, and only two major power blocs. NATO vs. the SovBloc; (briefly) America vs. the Japanese Co-Prosperity Sphere; latterly (in these times when the bell-shaped curve of economic empire is at maximum forty years wide) Europe, her client states in the old Eastern Bloc and the shaky democracy of Suid-Afrika vs. the emergent, vigorous culture of a Pan-Islam that had unified Arabia with North Africa, was ratifying probationary membership status from the Dardanelles to Srinagar, and was whistling political *come-hithers* to Sub-Saharan Africa and the new Confederation of Black American States. Saracens and Crusaders faced off across the Straits of Gibraltar.

"With me playing Charlton Heston strapped onto his horse?"

As ever, my filmic allusions were lost on the blind woman from Ghent. "Ideologically, we have no quarrel with Pan-Islam," she said. "It's our major trading partner; the new North African bourgeoisie keep most of France and Spain in work. We can't even accuse them of religious fundamentalism anymore: Sidi Ali in Riyadh brew the best lager beer in the world, probably. It's pure, old-fashioned imperialism. They want ours, we want theirs, and God or Allah help the nonaligned."

Meaning: violent guest-worker labor disputes in Spain, Portugal, and southern France had been traced to the Islamic-Socialist Al Haq group that Pan-Islam, eager to *rapproche* with its neighbor, had offered to terminate as a gesture of good faith. As Strasbourg's political strategists opined that détente might swing the nonaligned Beninian states into Cairo's fold, Al Haq must be eliminated by Europa, thus heightening diplomatic tension and counter-swinging the Benin States back to Europe and with them most of Tropical Black Africa. Thus, hazed out with free-gee tranqs and Chaotic Social Dynamics Theory, I fell on a suborbital parabola toward Marrakech and the vital cultural heart of the new Islam.

The red city between the desert and the snows had always seduced Westerners; now with the brilliance and sophistication of the lost Imperial days restored, it had joined the line of new Bohemias: Paris, Berlin, Swinging London, Greenwich Village, Kathmandu. Little surprise, therefore, to find flyposted to a wall in the old city that had stood since the days of the Cid the name, face, and floppy Mohican of Luka Casipriadin. A cartel of European industrials with taxes to avoid and North African markets to placate had culturally exchanged her via the Pan-Islam Arts Directorate and commissioned a room at some undisclosed site in the old city. She had rented a house there: Intelligence supplied address/phone/fax/ e-mail and gave me a suitable rendezvous: the Mermaid Café, *the* place for expatriate Europeans, which I took to mean Intelligence Division Junior Staffers. I left messages on all available media. She came to the Mermaid Café as the trees were filling with migratory birds and the streets with Marrakech's loud, confident, beautiful young people. She wore black, with lots of silver.

"You do know, Ethan, that this place is so noncredible it's death to my street-cool to be seen even walking past?" The year and a half between Mermaid Café and San Francisco executive suite might never have existed. The tap behind her ear obliged with the Arabic for a bottle of wine. "Fucking muck, but I'll say this for them, they have the best jukebox in the city, if you're into unfettered schmaltz and masochistic nostalgia in strict 4/4 time." We tried both. She was right on both. We danced at pupil-dilation distance until the place filled up with drunk Finns roaring *Suooooomi!* at the tops of their voices. ("Proves my point, Eth"), whereupon she whirled me into the neon-and-laser-lit labyrinth of the old city ("I've got a mind-map hardjiggered into my medulla, otherwise I'd never find my way home at night") between the street-sleepers and the knife-sharp *jeunesse* in Italian leathers on fluorescent biopower Vespa mopeds ("I always envied my mother hitting puberty in the Swinging Sixties with all that monochrome and PVC; here, I think I can understand what it felt like") through corridors splattered with the still-dripping scars of spray-bomb rumbles between rival political/theological/ artistic/philosophical/scientific groups ("Here, youth matters; they really believe they have the power to change the world, make it better, fairer, more civilized, more beautiful, more wild") past ranks of fast-food booths and stalls selling bootleg CDs and Dutch meatware and better-than-original ersatz Cartier accessories and Chanel smell ("What makes it so appealing, so exciting to a Euro stegosaur like me is that the media of expression haven't yet been usurped by accountants. The Almighty Ecu isn't the be-all and end-all; whatever your voice: music, poetry, flat-art, 3-D, time-base, VR, art-narcs, writing, drama, you can get heard") into the sweat and heat and firelight of the Square of Souls ("It's all one big underground, Eth. Everybody's free. Come on and I'll show you this crazy-priest, some kind of sufi, he can look right into people's souls and slay them in the spirit; they just keel right over backward. Fucking amazing. When did you last see that down at the Pompidou Center, or Covent fucking Garden?"). And the fires burned and the jugglers juggled and the crazy-priests preached and slew men's souls while still in their bodies, but she did not sleep with me.

In the morning I went to destroy Al Haq. My contact was a member of the Islamic University Political Science department, into which Al Haq's cell structure was known to be linked. As an ex-pat, Dr. Prawal was wont to lunch daily at the same Bangladeshi restaurant; there I waited, at the farthest, darkest table, and watched him pick fastidiously at chick peas and *lobia* beans and tap his feet to Politically Correct Delta *dhangra*. I let him work his way through to coffee before sending him the note I had printed out in a cubicle in the men's toilet.

It read: *Go to the red-haired man with the silk tie with Curtiss C3 biplanes on it.* Printed, of course, in Malkhut.

"Excuse me, do I know you?" They never understand why they do what the fracter makes them do. Some strange compulsion.

"You don't," I said, and pushed a second note across the table to him. The Malkhut Arabic read: *Tell me everything you know about Al Haq.* When he had finished, I thanked him civilly and with the Hokhmah, the Angel of Forgetting, took away everything after his departure from the Politics and Social Studies Unit that afternoon. Then I went to wait with the bad wine and the blue music in the Mermaid for Luka. That was the night she took me to the dog pit and in the blood and meat and shit and death I refused to see any analogy to what I had done in the name of political expediency to fifty people in as many countries.

Now that I had been given his name and face, I studied Mohammed Bedawi, Al Haq's instigator and leader, as closely as a red-haired man in a russet city may. On Friday he left the city in a red Séat Albéniz and I followed in a hire-company Peugeot along dirt roads lined with billboards extolling Islamic Unity and advertising French *cañabarillos* through well-watered truck farms into the foothills of the Atlas. The road threw itself in loops and hairpin bends across the mountainsides. He stopped at a mountain village unchanged but for the satellite dishes, solar generators, and Toyota pickups in a thousand years. After exultantly greeting his family, he went with the men to prayer while the women prepared a meal. A hologram of a local *sidi*, pale in the sharp mountain air, hovered above the square tower of the village mosque. A farmer I asked told me Bedawi came here to pray with his family every Friday. I thanked him, and took away his memory of ever having met a red-haired Euro.

Luka was waiting for me at the Mermaid Café.

"Something to show you," she said and, taking my gloved hand in her gloved hand, whirled me off into the old city she loved so much. "Behold, *Purgatorio*," she announced, and pushed me through the low wooden door into the room she had created. *Purgatorio*; where failure and inadequacy and guilt are burned away. It was harrowing. It was ecstatic. It was a long luxurious plunge into the heart of darkness. It was sex with angels. It was astonishing and horrifying and beautiful and monstrous and disgusting and sad and shocking and funny and sickening and it did not touch me. It could not touch me. Some failures and guilts lie too deep for purgation.

All that next week while I prepared the termination, I could not avoid the impression that Luka had made that small room-sized hell for me.

"I wish you could touch me," she said one evening as we sat on wrought-iron chairs in the fern-filled courtyard garden of her house. Dressed in something black and sleeveless, she smoked Black Cats and practiced aromatic smoke-rings. "I want to feel your hands. I want your hands to feel me. Take off the gloves."

"You know I can't." I borrowed a draw or two on her thin brown *cañabarillo*. "It's not safe."

"Can't. Won't. You've always worn gloves. Emotional gloves. Touch not and be not touched. What are you so afraid of, Ethan?"

"I'm not afraid."

Suddenly, she had taken my wrists in her hands.

"But you are, Ethan. Afraid, and cold." Then she cried, honest, full tears. "I love you. You hurt me. What can I do? Nothing. There's nothing I can do. It has to be you, Ethan. If you want. I'll always be here, you'll always be able to find me, but you have to choose."

Did she know me so little that she had forgotten that with me it could never be either/or, but both/and?

Friday came. A trip to the main dealer had confirmed that full in-car office systems were standard on the Mark Six Séat Albeñiz Bedawi drove; Marrakech directory inquiries obligingly supplied the car's e-mail code. Thus equipped, I drove the rented Peugeot to a pretty spot I had noticed the previous week on the other side of the valley from a particularly precipitous section of the mountain road. There I waited. I listened to New Wave *rai*. I ate a bag of prickly pears. When I saw the Mark Six Séat Albeñiz as a red dot in the ochre shatteredness of the Atlas, I fetched the portable fonefax. As the red Séat started the hairpin ascent, I connected a pocket Olivetti/ICL Mark 88 bioprocessor to the modem. A gasoline truck-trailer combo came grinding down the steep grade. As the red Séat passed the booth where I had bought the prickly pears, I loaded the Sefirah disk and keyed in the fracter commit code. As the car rounded the curve before the very special drop, I called the number directory inquiries had given me, thumbed *transmit*, and rezzed Keter the Destroying Angel up on his onboard display. From my high place I watched the Mark Six Séat Albeñiz veer toward the oncoming tanker, slew back across the road, crash through the low, drystone wall, and fall with wonderful balletic slowness to detonate in a blossom of flame on the rocks and scrub of the shadowy valley floor. I watched the gas combo stop dead, the driver leap down and stare for a full minute before running down the road, gesticulating wildly, toward the prickly pear booth. On my return to Marrakech I booked a seat on a shuttle to Malaga, packed, paid, and left, without explanation, without a note, without one good-bye for Luka.

Some dragons are too large, weigh too heavily on the landscape to be slain, however deserving of death they may be. Europa, the she-dragon, sprawling across a continent with ski resorts in her mountainous spines, eyes hidden behind red glasses while she seeks virgin nations to lunch upon, is perhaps more deserving of dispatch than many others, but even my Keter hand could not deliver shock enough to burn out its huge, slow, many-brained nervous system. But this saint may perhaps break the chain that binds it to the dragon's finger.

In the courtyard garden: early bird song, in darkness dawning. *Hurry up now, it's time.* I lay down the scissors, take up my weapons, and go to meet my enemy.

A bicycle is a friend in a way that an automobile can never be. A car can be a lover: sophisticated, complex, temperamental, but one wrong step and the affair is over. The bicycle is simple, undemanding, faithful, but as with any friendship, you must work at it, maintain it, repair it where necessary, spend time with it, get to know its character. I have come to love this green and purple Dirt Wolf MTB. We started strangers, newly introduced by Mas at the ferry terminal at Osaka, but through mutual misunderstandings—pulled muscles, stripped chains, skinned elbows, dented wheels—we have established a relationship. From the Tanazaki-ya to Tosa Securities headquarters is only fifteen kilometers through dull teleburbia but the pleasure of having a good machine between your thighs, responsive to your touch and need, is a transcendent joy. Following the instructions I pried out of the one akira capable of supplying them, I turn off the tree-lined avenue of Affluent Telecommuter Houses with Slightly Less Affluent Telecommuter Homes built in their gardens and Even Less Affluent Telecommuter Apartments built in *their* gardens ad infinitum onto the private lane and so come to the gates of Graceland. Cast-aluminum treble clefs surmounted by Spyball cameras and minded by ToSec cops in replica Mr. Nudie suits, even down to the Fender guitars embroidered on the lapels: what else can it be?

It is always dangerous when your enemy has a sense of humor. Ask Batman.

I ride up to the gates—the guards growl—dismount (stay there, good and faithful servant), and lift my naked right hand to the security cameras.

"Hi there." It is not quite as nonchalant in Japanese as I would like it to be. "Let me in." And the gates of Graceland open before me. I slap a peel-off/stick-on biodecay label over the camera lens, fracter side down. Binah the time-freezer will take care of whoever is on the monitors. The astonished guards reach for Fiuzzis in inside pockets. Too slow, beefboys. I rip the extruded fracter from the demon box hooked to my belt, slap it to my helmet. And disappear as their pieces come level with my heart. Lost Acres: 'Becca's Blind Spot fracter. Anything within a two-meter radius vanishes as the perception centers close up space around it. While they are still milling around like a duet for Laurel and Hardy sumo wrestlers, I pop up and slap a couple of Binahs over their Ray·Ban data shades. Frozen. Playing statues. A moment to cover my rear with a second Lost Acres on the back of my helmet, and I am ready to continue following the raked gravel drive between its dark banks of rhododendrons. The pairs of guards I encounter never stand a chance against an enemy that can step out of their blind spot and blast them into no-time with freeze fracters. Pray Lord Daishi they don't have extended sensory rigs on those shades of theirs; I'm as naked as Lady Godiva in infrared, and as vulnerable. The big fear is dogs like the ones I fought in the cane field. Lost Acres won't fool their noses and to use Keter as I did that time I'll have to step out of the blind spot.

I cut through the rhododendrons onto an expanse of beautifully striped lawn punctuated with twice-life-size busts of Buddy Holly, Eddie Cochrane, Chuck Berry, Patsy Kline, Little Richard, Bill Haley. Elvis. Rock'n'roll heaven. Gene-tweaked muntjak deer graze among the greats. Surreal, but at least dwarf deer preclude cybercanines. Beyond the lawn, a swath of yellow gravel, beyond the yellow gravel, an antebellum Scarlett O'Hara mansion. The only indication that I am still in Japan and not wet-dream Amerika is the ToSec thunder-eagle riding the portico.

I glimpsed a guitar-shaped pool around the side.

My activities have not gone unnoticed—I did not imagine I would gain the *sanctus sanctorum* unchallenged. Enforcers stand around on the gravel, automatics in hands, eyes fixed on the sky as if expecting an attack by Superman. Nothing for it but to screw my courage to the sticking point, make a fast, low, mad run across the noisy, treacherous gravel and hope to make it to the door before they empty their magazines into the sound of my footsteps. Go for it, Ethan, *go* . . .

They do not even turn. This is too easy. Suspiciously too easy. Inside Graceland, I slam and bolt the door and tear off my face of invisibility. I have a different weapon here: Gevurah, the destroying fear of God. As I move through the corridors like divine wrath, sending those I meet fleeing from me screaming in terror, I discover that Graceland is an enigma within a joke. The magnolias-and-mint-juleps exterior is a hollow shell of offices and access ways; within, glimpsed through windows and ventilators, is a mansion-sized space roofed with glass and walled with what I can only describe as three-story videowalls. Hundreds of televisions; thousands. On the polished wood floor stand four Neo-Shinto torii gates, each facing a cardinal point. Between them is a shoji-walled tile-roofed Daishi Hall.

For the first time, my confidence—my arrogance—falters. Lord Daishi walk with me.

Do I imagine, or are the massed televisions filled with faces?

Too dangerous to leave lying around: I hold the Fear demon in the flame from my silver Zippo until it crisps and curls in death. Then I mount the steps to the door signed ADMINISTRATION AND ACCOUNTS.

"Good morning," I announce to the assembled secretaries submanagers PAs account executives and two punky but cute kids in VR bodygloves. "Please don't be afraid." Not quite the smooth purr of James Mason in *The Wicked Lady*, but they look at me and I catch their spirits in my right hand. "The instructions I am about to download into your workstations are absolute and cannot be countermanded, is that clear?" Even the boys in the film-circuit suits bow. I've been looking forward to this since the idea came to me on the ride up from the Tanazaki-ya. "You will arrange to have every ToSec accountholder paid the equivalent of five years premiums. You will place all privately held stock in the company on the Pacific Rim market. You will then divide what is left among yourselves, leave the building as quickly as possible, and take a lengthy holiday." The demon box says it all so much more eloquently in Fracter Kanji onscreen but every guy ought to have a chance to play Robin Hood riding through the glen once in his life. Steal from the rich, give to the poor? It may not be FX courtesy Industrial Light and Magic, but the humble tap dance of Qwerty keys that signals the true destruction, the economic dismemberment, of Tosa Securities. If I go now with my hands full of white heat it is purely personal.

Double doors open without command from me; I advance silently across the polished wood floor toward the heart of Graceland. Silently, the banked walls of television screens blizzard and fill with faces; men, women, old, young. Children. Westerners; Euros, Americans, not many. Among the faces, the odd blank screen swept by momentary flurries of images with the eye-wrenching flavor of fracters. The pillars of the torii gate are studded with soul-taps.

Tosa Securities' dream of empire is created and upheld by the hands of the dead. Stolen souls. Enslaved memories. Dozens—hundreds, perhaps—of expert systems to manage and monitor and administer and operate and observe. Tireless. Constant. Vigilant. Eternal. If the dead are its digits, its senses, who—what—is its guiding intelligence? The door to the Daishi Hall swings open. What else to do, but enter?

Hanging brass lamps illuminate the serene features of hundreds of Buddhist saints lining the walls; I recognize Kannon, Dainichi, Binzuru forever denied Buddhahood because of his fondness for strong drink. The place of the central image on the altar is occupied by what looks like a suit of antique armor with a television set for a head.

"Life imitates *anime*?" I say in English, advancing between the Boddhisattvas and Boddhidharmas. The suit of armor, I see now, is built onto the frame of a ubiquitous Dornier Industrial Robot, identical to Luka's familiar, Oddjob, that guided us through the Californian undersoul. I close until I can see my face reflected whole in the blank television screen beneath the swooping winged helmet. "Not so very far away there are people eating their breakfast and watching the early news."

The blade is a terrifying blur of silver; a steel wind in my face; held poised, still, ready to strike, as my left hand is poised, still, ready.

"It could as easily have been your head, Mr. Ring." English. Received Pronunciation. Idiomatic. Perfect as only the top-line taps can be.

I begin to understand. I begin to be very afraid.

"It could as easily have been yours." I close my left hand.

"Somehow I doubt it, Mr. Ring."

Like an old Ray Harryhausen animation, the samurai-machine steps down from the altar, needle feet clicking, clicking on the wooden floor. Two of its four arms terminate in short, sharp blades. Childhood nightmares: television memories of spidercrabs dredged up from the floor of the Sea of Japan, five meters of clicking, chitinous, spindly armor. Fighting primal revulsion, I give ground.

"All done with computers, isn't it?" I shout to the Boddhisattvas and Boddhidharmas, to the massed personas in their television screens. To anything that will hear. "How did you die?"

"Cancer, Mr. Ring. Of course. Some say that the fact that it forewarns you is a grace, a time to square yourself with the Buddha or your ancestors or Allah and find dignity. Not me, Mr. Ring. But then I've always been an exception to the common rules. I found anger instead; anger that the body I had trained rigorously to obey my will should so fatally betray me; anger that my ambition, my work, should become the ambition and work of others less able than I. Anger.

"The death itself was quite painless. My soul-tap was downloaded into the simulator, my children and employees were suitably mournful, I became a simulacrum, an animated memory. Then the strange thing occurred, Mr. Ring, that I cannot properly explain to you, or anyone, because it involves the very unexplainability of self and otherness. I came back to life. I became more than recorded memories, passive, dead. I became aware, Mr. Ring, I became sentient, active, alive. I like to imagine it was my anger, the strength of my indignation that would not die and was reincarnated in the machine. Certainly, it was anger and the acquisitive urge that inspired me to build my company that led me to raid those other simulacra with whom I shared the simulator, and subjugate them, and mold them into tools, weapons, with which I could wrest control of the company away from my heirs. Their dismay when they found that the systems would not obey them, when they saw my face on their monitors!"

Another few steps across the wooden floor.

"Every nation has a date, Mr. Ring, a place, a time when everyone remembers exactly what they were doing, because it is the exact moment of cultural synthesis. With you it is the death of Elvis Presley, the destruction of the *Challenger*. With us it is the early morning light over Hiroshima. I saw that light, Mr. Ring. I saw the back rain of the dust and ashes of Empire. And I saw that Empire rebuild herself, proudly shake off American paternalism, take on that Empire, defeat it. If now we have passed from center stage to the lesser roles, I have no regret; the bit players may yet outperform the headline stars."

This house; this cultural schizophrenia; this Neo-Imperial adventure: I understand. Behind the white-painted geisha mask, the soul lies unchanged, unchanging, unchangeable.

"And now you're taking up the sword of Mishima."

"It requires a special nobility to disembowel yourself on a hotel balcony, but Mishima was an idealist, and idealists are fools. We Takedas are pragmatists: I merely want what was always mine to begin with; my lands, my respect, my name."

"If it had been for the soul of Japan, I could have understood," I say. "But you're just one more fucking little *daimyo*."

"Who wants, and will have, your head, Mr. Ring."

The blade moves. This time I am ready. My right hand is held up before me.

"I don't think so, Mr. Takeda."

"*Lord* Takeda, if you please. And, as I have said before, I do think so."

The arc of the cut passes so close, my reflex recoil so slow, that I feel the kiss of the steel across my throat. The samurai-robot clicks into combat stance; one blade raised high, the other drawn back for the killing thrust.

*Blood* warm on my fingers. I stare at my right hand disbelievingly.

Impossible. Impossible. *Impossible.*

Left hand. Chaos hand. Death hand. The backs of my knuckles are pressed against my face. *Die, you diseased fuck.*

"It is written, Mr. Ring, that the way of victory lies in *becoming your enemy*," says the cultured BBC accent. He speaks? He sees Keter and lives? How? *How?* I hardly hear his words for the blood surging red in my brain. "I know you, Mr. Ring. Do you think your European masters would have let their most valuable, most powerful weapon go cycling gaily over hill and dale unchaperoned?"

"They had you watch me?"

"We were contacted by the European embassy while you were still shopping for bicycles in Tokyo with your animator friend. Since you stamped your albums at Temple One, ours has been the unseen presence accompanying you on your pilgrimage. We Two, Pilgrims Together. You did manage to evade us at Tokushima but we caught up with you again at Temple Nineteen and put up the Hiyasa checkpoint to lock on. I am still not certain whether it was unfortunate or serendipitous that you left the Approved Tourist Route at Aki. If you hadn't, you might never have encountered the dog patrol and I would never have seen exactly why your European masters value you so highly."

Those dead televisions, those semi-fracters blizzarded with interference Someone had been monitoring those dogs, as I had suspected, but no one living.

"Had I been observing you through purely visual channels, my persona would be as hopelessly disrupted as your other victims. But I am hunting you with subtler senses—infrared, sound, motion sensors ..."

"My head does not come easily, Mr. Takeda." Europeans too can read the masters. *Strike in an unexpected manner*, writes Miyamoto Musashi. Robot limbs are strong but the muscle joints are fragile. Do my enemy's sensors register a warp of heat, a flicker of digits as I dart between the splayed legs, wrench down the upraised blade arm, break its joint across my knee, and, as the second blade comes blurring toward me, cleave it cleanly at the first joint with the stolen sword?

More things than tourist-talk Japanese in my plastic socket.

"It is a mistake to rely on only one weapon," I quote, gasping, heart hammering.

"Quite," says the Takeda-thing. "But you are not the only one who can play the Scissor-Paper-Stone Game." The faceless television opens its single eye. It is only because I once saw its face and survived that the Keter fracter does not cinder my eyes in my head. Even the split second of recognition and reaction is like lightning earthing down my spine. What? Where? Feel. Feel. Wooden floor. Closed. Keep your eyes closed. Feel. My quivering fingers touch the carved foot of a wooden Boddhisattva. I hear clicking, mincing footsteps. My enemy, closing to destroy me. But the battle is more than Ethan Ring's personal nemesis now. A ToSec in possession of the passwords and commands recorded on the soul-tap wired into my skull and loose in the world with the fracters in its hands: there is no imagining how this drama of history will end.

"I can see you, Mr. Ring. Can you see me?"

You cannot afford one glance; for if you have just handed it Malkhut the Obedience fracter ... Keter you might survive through familiarity, but an unrefusable order to slit your own stomach ...

Movement sensors. Infrared. And, in my belt pouch, the can of spray lubricant I used on that troublesome gearshift ... I check with my fingers for my cigarette lighter. Work, fingers, fuck you, work. Get that top off. Christ, I can hear it, stepping across the floor. Get away, you bastard, get away. I feel my way along the Buddhas. *Forgive me, Lord Daishi.* The oil spray ignites into a gout of fire; I wave my improvised flamethrower over the wooden images, sending the Buddhas up in a roar of enlightenment. I can no longer hear the sure click, step of the Takeda-robot. In the shelter of my arms, I snuff out my fire, spray thick, black oil over my wraparound MTB shades.

"Right, you bastard."

Fools, fighting in a burning house ...

"Impressive, Mr. Ring."

The voice, too close, too near ... Multijointed fingers clamp around my throat, squeeze blood from the hairline wound, push me back toward the blazing Buddhas. I hammer with the base of my spray can, but robot fingers lock onto my glasses; lift them. My one free hand sprays pure blackness into the place I hope the screen to be. Plastic fingers spasm; I snap joints like crab legs, wriggle free. Do I, dare I, dare I, do I? One glance. I dare. I do.

The spray has blacked out the left side of the winged helmet and three quarters of the glowing screen. *Namu Daishi Henjo Kongo!* I must act quickly, decisively, before Takeda reformats the fracter into a smaller screen.

One glance can contain the key to victory. On the rear of the carapace, exactly where I remember Luka had plugged the multiplex link transmitter into her Oddjob, is a fifteen-pin socket, standard issue on the Dornier Mark 15.

The Takeda-thing spins on its legs, hunting for a true image in the blur of infrared distractions but I am faster. In the instant before its motion sensors register, I am on top of it. The Daishi Hall is a hell of blazing Boddhisattvas and Boddhidharmas, but the demon box is off my belt, its adaptor pushed into the socket where the Takeda-thing cannot reach.

"You wanted the fracters," I shout over the roar of burning, the scream of fire alarms. "Then have them."

I press the DUMP DISK key.

COMMIT CODE? asks the demon box.

My fingers, numbs from Keter-shock, miskey. A crushing agony in the back of my neck; robot fingers trying to tear head and spine from my body.

WHAT I TELL ...

The other hand is spidering on broken fingers around the base of my skull, feeling, questing, feeling ...

WHAT I TELL YOU THREE ...

A chitinous finger screws, screws into the plastic vulva of my taphead socket. The pain is delirious, but nothing to what it will be if Lord Takeda succeeds in firing a macrovolt charge through my cerebellum.

WHAT I TELL YOU THREE TIMES ...

I am burning. I am dying.

IS ...

He is scraping out the inside of my skull, sucking down my soul, swallowing me.

TRUE.

COMPLETE FRACTER SYSTEM DOWNLOAD EFFECTED says the demon box. And in the same instant, Lord Takeda's grip on my soul is released. Pain ceases, I roll clear. By the light of a hundred burning Buddhas, I see the Takeda-thing, legs locked into a pyramid, arms out at its sides, rigid, while Marcus's Sefirah disk pours all the fear and all the joy and all the pain and all the annihilation and all the madness and all the healing and all the holiness and all the remembering and all the forgetting and all the highs and lows and peace and loathing and death in all the world through him.

"Burn in hell, you bastard!"

The pillars are alight, flames are running along the roof beams and trusses. The shoji walls have already gone. I have only moments before the roof comes down, but there are two last things to be burned in this fire ceremony. The heat and smoke force me down to crawl, choking, skin seared, across the floor to the fallen image of Kokuzo.

Once, Luka had videoed a young street preacher who used a large paschal candle as an allegory of hell. "One thousand ecus to anyone who will hold his finger in the flame for one minute!" he would harangue the Saturday shoppers. "One minute? No takers? How can you then contemplate an eternity of burning in hell!"

But some things must be contemplated. Some hells must be embraced. I press my hands to the glowing wood. The pain blows away every thought, everything except the need to stop it, stop it, stop it. But I cannot. I cannot. *Namu Daishi Henjo Kongo Namu Daishi Henjo Kongo Namu Daishi Henjo Kongo Namu Daishi Henjo Kongo.* Hold them. I watch my hands blacken, *hold them* and split, *hold them* and smoke, and burn, and crisp to obscene scraps of charred gristle. *Hold them.* I hold them until very trace and line of the things that were engraved there are burned away. Only then, transfigured with pain, do I run from the Daishi Hall as the roof falls in a gout of flame on the blazing, melting Takeda-thing, run out between the smoking torii gates beneath the glass roof of the hollow Graceland that cracks in the sudden uprush of heat and shatters into dozens of tesselated Fuller-hexagons, all falling down, all drifting down, all coming down, raining down on me.

The legend attached to the small, un-numbered *bangai* a morning's walk through beautiful country beyond Temple Twenty-seven is one of the most unusual of the whole pilgrimage. As the Daishi was passing

through this part of Shikoku he met a trader leading
a packhorse laden with dried salt trout. Kobo Daishi
asked for the gift of one fish but years of sin had
hardened the fish trader's heart, and not even sparing
the smallest and least fish, he urged his horse on. Im-
mediately, it was struck with paralyzing colic and the
man, remembering he had heard that a great holy man
was abroad on the island, went back to beg the
Daishi's forgiveness. The Daishi handed the trader his
begging bowl and told him to fill it with water from
a nearby spring and give it to the horse. This he did,
and the horse was at once restored. In gratitude, the
trader offered the Daishi all his load of fish but the
saint would accept only one, the smallest and least,
which he put into the spring, prayed, and immedi-
ately, it was returned to life. The fish trader built a
hermitage by that spring, which over the centuries has
become this Buddhist Temple. Fish still swim in the
pool fed from the spring; the monks are keen to show
visitors the marks behind their heads, on either side
of their backs, and on the tails that are the prints of
the Daishi's fingers.

On their instructions, I am to bathe my hands
twice a day—dawn and sunset—in the restoring waters. I cannot say I have felt any great blessing, perhaps what benefit there is exists in the physical
exercise of walking down to the pool and the spiritual
grace of watching slow creatures in deep, clear liquid.
Whatever, my nurse assures me that when I do go to
bathe, the bioassay lines on the robot that follows me
like a bad conscience dip into smoother, more tranquil configurations.

They are a kind and true people, this reclusive
brotherhood of homosexual monks. They live the

spiritual life with the natural, liquid grace of a trout in water. Few things are more attractive than natural saintliness, few things rarer to find. Many of them are men who have stepped away from the professional world but feel that their sexual orientation precludes them from the regular spiritual orders; the Trout Brook Temple brothers are renowned among the few who know of their existence as strong gentle healers, razor-sharp accountants, and fearsome lawyers. After Mas found me in the chaos and destruction of Graceland and brought me back to the Tanazaki-ya, the Tanazakis sent for the brothers of Salt Trout Temple, knowing that they possessed both the power to save me and keep me hidden from those who might be interested in the man who single-handedly destroyed Tosa Securities Incorporated. Like all men of spiritual integrity, the brothers have little interest in the processes of history.

While the major players in Japan's unfolding act of kabuki manipulate and maneuver in the vacuum left by the sudden collapse of ToSecInc, I become acquainted with my new hands. The plastic skin is a little disconcerting, especially its shocking, terminal junction with the pale, freckled Ethan-skin of my wrists but Brother Saigyo, my loving nurse, gives me daily assurances that beneath the stiff, clawlike carapaces, new skin is growing, thickening, laying down layer upon layer, minute by minute, hour by hour, day by day. Pigment, hair, nails, fingerprints, all will be exactly as before thanks to the miracle of accelerated regeneration.

"I hope not," I say but I have never yet, and never will, let Brother Saigyo into my little joke. I hope not; I think not. When the medical robot unseals these plastic shells and I dip them into the Daishi's water, the sight of them may run slivers of neurasthenic shock into my brain, but they feel good, they feel clean.

"Visitor for you," says Brother Saigyo, grinning impishly. I am not surprised, I have been expecting this visit since I came out of anesthesia in a blissful high of pain and remembered what Mas had said that night in the Tanazaki-ya. "Will you go down, or shall I send her up?"

"Send her up," I say, comfortable, secure with my beer, newspapers, diskperson, and robot familiar on the pilgrim hostel veranda. I watch the way she moves up the flagged path through the funeral plinths, brushing the stones with her hands, past the sub-chapels, feeling the soft stroke of pine needles through her fingers, the unconscious sensuality of everything she ever did, her unfettered spontaneity, and it is like a nail in my heart. She mounts the veranda steps, one, two, three, four, surveys my empty beer cans, newspapers, disks, robot.

"Well, you got a long way, didn't you?"

Black skirt, long, fringed, and a-jingle with Indian bells; black Docs; black sleeveless poloneck. Much silver. That ludicrous crest of black hair she could never keep out of her eyes.

"You get as far as the Daishi permits you," I say. "This far, this pilgrimage, I only have grace enough for twenty-seven and a half temples."

We embrace; she wraps her long skinny bare arms with their jangling silver bangles around me; I feel the quick shiver of bare emotion. I do some sort of half hug, all forearms and elbows, strangely reluctant to touch her with my plastic hands.

"How are they, Eth?" I show her. She looks disgusted.

"Jesus, Eth. I told Mas I'd foot the bill. I mean, make the appropriate contribution to temple funds. They're sharp boys, these monks. Mas won't hear of it, he says he makes five times what I do and will never miss it, which is probably true, but I'm going to do it anyway."

"They'll be as good as they were before," I say. "Almost." Then: "They're gone, Luka. That was why I did it. It was the only way to get rid of them. Burn them out."

"It was always heroes and angels with you, wasn't it, Eth?" She leans back against the veranda rail, stretches her arms as far as they will go to either side along the knotted wood.

"The disk is gone too, Luka. It burned in the fire. All gone. The fracters, Marcus's dream, burned."

"Mas says when he found you you were muttering something over and over and over."

"What?"

" 'I'm sorry, Marcus; I'm sorry, Marcus.' Over and over and over."

"Luka."

She smiles out at me from underneath that ludicrous hair.

"I'm free. I died in the fire with the Takeda simulacrum. Ethan Ring does not exist anymore. A closed file in a gray office in Ghent."

"Shit, Ethan, I don't want to run all my life. I've got better things to do ..."

"You won't, Luka. I'm sure of it. Without the fracters, they have no use for me."

"Well, if they change their minds and decide they want you back after all, they'll have to come through me." She looks over her shoulder at the temple garden.

"I'm fucking starving, Eth. I've been on the go since before breakfast. You know, Mas wouldn't tell me where you were? I had to meet him in Yawatahama and let him bring me here. *Mondo secreto.* What did you do? The whole country is going mad out there."

"I'm pretty much out of the world here," I say. "Thankfully. I can get you something to eat but they're pretty strict interpretation Buddhist diet-wise. Vegetables, no grains."

"Suits me."

"Eat what I eat."

"Become you."

"Is that what you want?"

For the first time we dare eye contact.

"Yes it is. Yes."

She pulls me to her, runs her tongue over my red-stubbled scalp.

"That fabulous, fabulous hair," she mourns; then, intimate, in my ear, sly: "How are they about other things?"

"To the brothers, it's a spiritual grace. As long as there's love in it."

"I think that could be arranged."

She takes my destroyed hands in her hands, lifts her arms high, opens them wide.

"They're gone, Luka. They won't come back. But sometimes, if the light is right, in the early morning, or at sunset, I think I can see something written there, under the plastic."

She freezes, every muscle prepared for a final, killing act of betrayal. In the same instant she chooses to trust me.

"What do they say, Ethan?"

" 'Emon Saburo Reborn.' "

"And are you going to tell me what that means?"

Our hands come together at the bottom of the circle of air.

"Some year, Luka, some year."

# Thanks and Acknowledgments

FIRST AND ALWAYS, TO MY WIFE TRISH, WHOSE CON-
tribution to all my work is far greater than she can ever
imagine, and especially to the H.N.D. Design Commu-
nication Class of '92 at the University of Ulster Faculty
of Art and Design in Belfast, whose lives, times, and
works form the warp and weave of this story. Those
who deserve thanks know who they are; I consider myself honored to have been worthy of the Award of the
Silver Tinsel, signifying Honorary Membership of this
rare body.

Two books are the spiritual parents of this work.
Oliver Statler's *Japanese Pilgrimage* (Picador; London,
1984) first brought the Shikoku pilgrimage to my attention; if I've sampled it mercilessly, I hope I've done so
in the spirit of a tribute to an underappreciated master-
piece. Likewise, acknowledgment is also due Jan
Wozencroft's *The Graphic Language of Neville Brody* (Thames
and Hudson; London, 1988), required reading not only
on the undervalued art of typography from which the
idea of Authoritative Typefaces was extrapolated, but

also as one of the clearest apologias of the '70s–'80s punk ethos.

Thanks: to Gary Gibson and Mike Cobley, who don't know it, but introduced me to the wonderful world of Japanese *anime*; to Charles Stross, for an idle comment about computer animation systems; to Betsy Mitchell for faith in things unseen, etc., and the Religious Views of Life; to Robert M. Pirsig for long-standing inspiration: all fellow pilgrims together.

*Namu Daishi Henjo Kongo!*